For fourteen years now *Perry Rhodan* has been acknowledged to be the world's top-selling science fiction series. Originally published in magazine form in Germany, the series has now appeared in hardback and paperback in the States.

Over five hundred *Perry Rhodan* clubs exist on the Continent and *Perry Rhodan* fan conventions are held annually. The first Perry Rhodan film, *SOS From Outer Space*, has now been released in Europe

The series has sold over 150 million copies in Europe alone.

Also available in the *Perry Rhodan* series

ENTERPRISE STARDUST
THE RADIANT DOME
GALACTIC ALARM
INVASION FROM SPACE
THE VEGA SECTOR
THE SECRET OF THE TIME VAULT
THE FORTRESS OF THE SIX MOONS
THE GALACTIC RIDDLE
QUEST THROUGH SPACE AND TIME
THE GHOSTS OF GOL
THE PLANET OF THE DYING SUN
THE REBELS OF TUGLAN
THE IMMORTAL UNKNOWN
VENUS IN DANGER
ESCAPE TO VENUS

W W Shols

PERRY RHODAN 16

Secret Barrier X

Futura Publications Limited
An Orbit Book

An Orbit Book

First published in Great Britain in 1976
by Futura Publications Limited

Copyright © Ace Books 1972 (*Secret Barrier X*)
Copyright © Forrest J Ackerman 1972
(*Pursuit to Mars*)
Copyright © Oblique House and Clark
Publishing Co 1950 by permission of
Walter A Willis and the author's
agent. (*Swordsmen of Varnis*)
An Ace Book by arrangement with
Arthur Moewig Verlag.
This series was created by Karl-Herbert
Scheer and Walter Ernsting, translated by
Wendayne Ackerman and edited by
Forrest J Ackerman and Frederik Pohl

ISBN 0 8600 7900 7
Printed in Great Britain by
Richard Clay (The Chaucer Press) Ltd.,
Bungay, Suffolk
Futura Publications Limited
110 Warner Road, Camberwell, London SE5

Contents

1	Time Warp in Hell	7
2	Of Seals and Sorcerers	20
3	'Worse than Pirates'	33
4	'The Power in His Eyes'	47
5	Rhodan to the Rescue	66
6	Attack of the Tree-Lizard	79
7	The Carata Vampire Strikes	96
8	Jungle Warfare	107

This English edition dedicated to *Otis Adelbert Kline* Whose Grandon of Terra Once Had Grand Adventures on Venus too

1. TIME WARP IN HELL

'NO! NO! NO!

'We're *not* going back to Earth!

'We're going to remain right here in orbit around Venus!

'Have I made myself clear?'

The members of the Mutant Corps were cowed by Reginald Bell's emphatic orders. In Perry Rhodan's absence Bell was in command of the small band of people with super powers. They didn't always agree with his reasoning but they were loyal to their commander.

Bell was now in an exposed position. A failure could be in the offing. 'There's something wrong here,' he continued in an irritated voice, indicating the surface of Venus below with his index finger. 'No one in the service of the Chief of the New Power, no one who has sworn allegiance to Rhodan, can desert him when he's in deep trouble. You want to return to Earth – and how will he fare then? You know he's stuck down there, almost alone in the Venusian jungle crawling with deadly creatures and . . .'

'Okura will be with him. And Marshall and Thora, too,' a small but broad-shouldered, powerfully built mutant ventured to interject. It was Wuriu Sengu, the seer.

Bell cut him short. 'Thora took off in a ship alone. Or if anybody was with her it was only a robot. Rhodan, Marshall and Okura followed in a second rocket. We know that crazy positronic brain in the Venus fortress has suddenly gone blind or mad, activating the SBX against Perry himself who programmed it! The brain now repulses him with every technical means at its command and I've no reason to believe Perry and Thora have joined up with each other. All probabilities point to the likelihood that they've cracked up and are now helplessly exposed to the danger of this prehistoric planet.'

Sengu tried once more to dispel Bell's pessimistic views. 'The chief said something about the Arkonide woman being in good hands.'

Bell remained adamant. 'Strictly speaking, the chief said very little. He hardly had time for explanations. Our radio communication was cut off after only two minutes and all attempts since to get in touch with him have been negative. The robot brain in the Venus base has not only erected its 300 mile barrier but intercepts all radio transmissions between us and the stations below and prevents us from landing. Perry's wrist-set is useless. I don't think even our powerful ship-sender gets through. When the p.b. takes a defensive position, the damned machine does its job to the letter. Arkonide technology, men!'

The mutant Tanaka Seiko made a polite gesture. 'We've been through all these arguments before, sir. You admit yourself that we're powerless. So why do we have to remain in this orbit if we can't help our commander from here?'

Bell paused before replying. He scrutinized his listeners. (It was to his eternal regret that, because his

8

eyes were such a pale blue, his penetrating gaze never appeared as stern as he would have liked when he needed to enforce authority.)

Here stood the cream of his elite. They were the selected positive mutants of Rhodan's secret corps. Tanaka Seiko, for instance – endowed with an additional sense for receiving radio waves. Or seer Wuriu Sengu, who had no difficulties looking through solid objects.

Bell's gaze focused on Tako Kakuta. 'Yes, Tako, I mean you. Don't you agree that the positronic brain has completely failed to take one circumstance into consideration?'

'Are you referring to my capacity for teleportation, sir?'

'Of course! The brain machine in the Venus bulwark is 10,000 years old. I don't mean to say it's from the Stone Age; after all, it was constructed by an expedition of Arkonides whose technology was even then tremendously ahead of mankind today. But 10,000 years ago there weren't any mutants yet on Terra. This leads us to the sensible conclusion that the robot brain was not programmed for defense against teleportation.'

'You mean, I should ...' Tako Kakuta paused. He glanced hesitantly at the observation screen depicting the surface of Venus. Underneath the 60 yard sphere of *Good Hope V* the wild virgin landscape of the planet unfolded slowly, as in a time exposure. But details were not discernible. Now and then a gap in the dense blanket of clouds permitted a glimpse of the surface. Dark green, luxuriant forests; blue-green, sometimes even black shimmering oceans and grey-brown cliffs covered

9

with snow around the polar caps. The optical screen showed much less than the teleporter saw in his memory and fantasy. Tako had spent long weeks on Venus. He knew what awaited him in the labyrinth down there.

'Yes,' Bell nodded seriously. 'You should go down to make contact with Rhodan. Once you've found him, the rest is child's play. Together with the chief we're an invincible team and we'll accomplish what we set out to do. We'll transport Perry the quickest possible way into the fortress so that he can give new instructions to the brain.'

'That's obvious,' Sengu nodded optimistically. 'How come we didn't hit on this idea sooner?'

'We're too much inclined to accept an Arkonide energy barrier as absolute and infallible. Years of familiarity with Arkonide technology have created the unconscious conviction that it's nothing short of perfection. Get ready, Tako! It'll be just a skip and a jump for you.'

'The distance is ridiculously small, sir. I've been thinking for some time of taking a jump down there and would've done it on my own, if . . .'

'If what?'

'If it weren't for the jungle. I know the place. Even a teleporter can go astray in it after losing orientation. And without warning you run into all sorts of man-eating vermin. Even the quick reflexes of a teleporter are sometimes insufficient for flight from them.'

'Are you afraid?'

'I'm always a little afraid when going straight to hell. But this isn't what bothers me most. After all there are probably several thousand men down there who must be prepared at any moment to fight for their lives. But I need a concrete target. Unless it's determined exactly, I may have to teleport myself endlessly without having a chance to locate Rhodan.'

'Just let me worry about that! The shipboard positronic computer has collected all manoeuver data. We've also located Perry's position at his last radio transmission. He's situated exactly 72 miles west of the 200 mile wide ocean channel extending deep into the northern continent.'

'But this data isn't precise enough, sir.'

'I know. I didn't imply that you have to make your leap this very minute.'

Bell shoved the teleporter out of his way with a forceful hand and strode to the on-board positronic brain.

'Come here, all of you! Watch it that Tako and I make no mistakes. I'll guarantee you we'll fix Rhodan's position within 500 yards diameter at the most. Tako, if you don't fall into the arms of the chief, you'll have to go to the trouble of calling him.'

'Of course, sir!'

The evaluation of the stored data proceeded faster than anticipated. The servo-circuits of the brain reacted promptly. A projection of the Venus surface appeared on the millimeter grid. The picture was obtained on the basis of previous surveys.

More difficult was Tako Kakuta's individual adjustment to the problem, since he had to concentrate his mind on a precise aim and needed a concrete concept of the spot he endeavoured to reach through teleportation.

There were only very limited clues on Venus in this respect. The primeval forest appeared like an endless carpet from above presenting a rough impression of millions of similar geographical points.

Bell could sense Tako's difficulties. 'No sweat, my boy. I'll make it easier for you.' Saying which, he super-imposed the cartographic grid on the landscape. Although this was merely a visual aid, it proved to be a useful device.

'The orientation is very good,' Tako Kakuta said suddenly. Please don't change the cartographic grid, sir. Our course seems to be correct as well. We should reach the most favorable point for my departure in about 10 minutes.'

They checked their watches. In addition to the chronometers on board the ship, which corresponded with the Terrestrial calendar, they all carried the so-called Venus watches. Figured roughly, Venus rotated five times slower than Earth. Therefore a day on Venus was five times longer.

The point the positronic brain of the *Good Hope V* had ascertained as Rhodan's present position fell into the moving twilight zone. For their companions down on Venus a new morning had just dawned.

The Venus watches showed close to 78:00 o'clock.

Still five minutes to the most advantageous time to leap!

It was a time of silent waiting during which the tension rose. If anyone on board had misgivings about Kakuta's mission, he did not mention it. It could be possible that the teleportation of a mutant was the last chance for penetrating the barrier created by the robot brain in the Venus fortress.

Three minutes to go!

Wuriu Sengu, the seer, groaned in disgust. After he had stood for seconds in utmost concentration peering into the apparent void, he relaxed his body and threw himself with dismay into a chair.

Bell was angry at this demonstration of a pessimistic attitude since it could easily infect the others. 'What's the matter, Wuriu?'

'I've tried to recognize something under the mass of clouds. Of course, I can see more than you do. For you the surface of Venus is a bleak mantle of vapours and clouds yet for me it's a colourful and splendourous paradise. But we're more concerned now with detailed features and I can't make them out from this distance. About 20 miles south of the point specified by our computer is an almost barren high mesa. But the chief is most likely deep in the wild forest.'

'You mean, Wuriu, if he's smart, he'll try to reach the mesa?'

'Naturally! It offers the best protection against the unpredictable fauna of the planet.'

'You may be right. But the problems probably look more difficult down there than from up here. In any case, we can fully depend on the result of our positronic range finder. I'm convinced that the next 15 minutes will tell us more about the situation. All clear, Tako?'

One more minute to the right jump-off position.

The teleporter nodded.

In addition to his own equipment he carried an Arkonide operation-suit on his back. Everyone knew its

13

purpose: as soon as Kakuta located Rhodan, the suit would enable their commander to reach the Venus fortress without delay. There he had to revise the programming of the positronic brain. Thus the control of the New Power over the entire planet would once more be secured with one stroke. The Arkonide transport suits were a technical marvel in a class by themselves. They were light weight and could be worn comfortably over regular clothing. They transformed the wearer into a flying Icarus, since the built-in gravity neutralizer compensated the force of gravity of the average planet. By means of a lightwave deflector and energy protection screen anyone who put on such a suit also became invisible and unassailable.

The thought of these valuable aids for the impending operation restored the optimism of the crew. When Tako Kakuta handed the transport suit to Perry Rhodan, the episode of the shipwreck was cancelled.

'Ten seconds,' Reginald Bell called out. 'Be careful, Tako!'

'Here I go!'

The vanishing of a teleporter had become a daily occurrence in the life of Mutant Corpsmen. Nevertheless, they felt that the spectacle was mysterious and wonderful in this special case. A normal man leaves through a door or in an elevator but a teleporter just stands motionless on the spot. Purely by concentration of his mind he enters into a supra-dimensional field of existence which releases him again in his normal state at his destination.

Kakuta's image faded away moment by moment, gradually becoming more unreal, so that he gave the impression of disappearing in time.

Before they could count three, his place was empty.

'And now we must have a little patience,' Bell lectured. He intended to follow Wuriu and wait in a comfortable chair. However before he could sit down, a piercing scream caused him to spin around.

Wuriu had jumped up too and looked incredulously at the body writhing on the floor of the command center.

Tako Kakuta lay before them in convulsions of inexplicable torment. His scream had turned into a pitiful whimpering interrupted by violent coughing spells.

Ralf Marten, the tele-optician of the Mutant Corps, stepped back as Kakuta tried with closed eyes to grab his leg and pull him down with imploring, mad gestures.

'He's gone crazy!' Tanaka Seiko shouted. 'Let's get hold of him and tie him up. He doesn't know what he's doing!'

Obviously the teleporter didn't know what he was doing. Neither did the others know what they could do, since Kakuta was suffering from an unknown accident. He couldn't be treated as a culprit and a patient at the same time. Evidently he was more sick than 'crazy'.

'We've got to help him,' Marten declared, expressing both distrust and compassion in his attitude.

All those present had instinctively made a wide circle around Kakuta and now they began to take some remedial action.

'Ralf, concentrate on his brain!' Reginald Bell suggested. 'Tell me what he sees and hears!'

Ralf Marten's positive mutation enabled him to temporarily shut his own self out and receive through the eyes and ears of another the impression of the person thus 'taken over' but remaining completely unaware of what happened to him.

Marten concentrated his thoughts and assumed the typical rigid stance of the mutants. After a while he relaxed again and shook his head. 'Tako told me nothing at all. What he sees and hears can't be defined. He doesn't recognize us. His perception is confused as ...' Marten hesitated.

'Come on, out with it!' Bell urged. 'Are you telling us Tako is mad?'

The tele-optician nodded without conviction.

'That's what I was going to say. But I'm no physician. Don't pay too much attention to my impressions!'

'What the hell, Marten! You're only confusing the matter even worse. Tako's brain must mirror some reflexes. He was only outside the ship five seconds. He can't have become a total idiot in such a short time!'

The tele-optician shrugged his shoulders helplessly.

'I'm afraid, sir, I can't tell you how to proceed. If his brain really reflects his latest brief experiences, I can only say that the origin of his visual and acoustic impressions was also indefinable and absurd.'

'Don't bug him,' Wuriu Sengu counselled. 'After all, he's no telepath.'

'Thank you for your advice,' Bell replied, gnashing his teeth. 'Then we've got no other choice; we'll have to carry out Tanaka's suggestion and tie him up ... Wait a minute! He's calming down ...'

Tako Kakuta was suddenly lying still. Only his rapid

heavy breathing indicated his state of excitement. Finally he opened his eyes and stared at his friends without a sign of recognition.

'Let's be patient now,' Bell requested. 'Apparently his agitation is lessening. We can't relieve his pain until we know what the cause is.'

Bell approached the teleporter closer. 'Tako, what's the matter? Can't you talk to us?'

It took several more minutes before the little Japanese reacted to his surroundings for the first time. His mind seemed to get clearer. 'Reg, good heavens, why don't you help me?'

'I'll help you as soon as you explain to me what's wrong with you.'

'I've got pains.'

'Where at?'

'I'm hurting all over. My back, my head ... No man can stand three hours in that hell!'

The others looked at each other dubiously. Their glances seemed to insinuate that Tako must be insane.

'He was only three, maybe five seconds gone,' Tanaka Seiko stated. 'It's impossible that he landed on Venus in that time and left again.'

'But he must have experienced some horrible incident,' the captain commented. 'Let's lift him up and put him on the couch next door.'

First Bell kneeled down beside Tako and opened the zipper of his collar. It must have been a relief for Tako as he said distinctly, 'Thank you!'

They carried him into the next room without resistance. Tako was now completely passive and harmless. Obediently he swallowed a pain-relieving tablet.

'Are you feeling better?' Bell inquired.

'Yes, a little. Thank you!'

'Thank goodness! The way you carried on was enough to make us think you'd gone haywire. Do you already feel strong enough to give us a report?'

'There's not much to report. I didn't get down. It was impossible to get through.'

'Nobody expected you to get to Venus in the few seconds of your absence. No more than ...'

'Why are you always talking about a few seconds, sir?' Kakuta asked suspiciously. 'I was caught for many hours in an inferno before I was released again.'

'All right,' Bell soothed him. 'Let's not argue about minor points. What's really important is that you've made no mistakes.'

'How can a teleporter do anything wrong sir? I'm no more able to influence the process of teleportation than you can direct the manner in which your eyes and brain see. It's a natural gift and it functions according to its own laws.'

'H'm,' Bell thought out loud. 'If you haven't made any error, it won't do any good to repeat the experiment.'

'I'll be damned if I attempt it again! I beg your pardon, sir. Don't think I'm talking about insubordination. I can't explain it to you.'

'You referred to hell?'

'There's no other word to describe it. I was in a void and yet it was full of pain and torture. There can only be one explanation for it.'

'And that would be?'

'The robot brain repulsed me. The secret barrier

repels everything in whatever form it exists. This includes pure energy. After we were prevented from landing, a total interruption of our radio communications was imposed. Now we were shown that five-dimensional energy currents of teleportation are intercepted, too. I must have been transferred to a time field of higher order during my dematerialized state.'

'Which all boils down to what?'

'We're dealing with a discrepancy in the duration of my absence. All of you claim I was gone five seconds at the most. In my reality, however, my absence lasted considerably longer.'

As proof of his contention Tako raised his left arm, exhibiting the dial of his chronometer on his multi-purpose bracelet. 'My watch is two and a half hours fast. Isn't this valid proof?'

They agreed. From this moment on the crew of *Good Hope V* accepted with resignation the fact that they were unable to assist Perry Rhodan in the jungles of Venus. Rhodan and his companions were left to their own resources. They had to find the solution of their problems by using their wits.

2. OF SEALS & SORCERERS

John Marshall ran for his life.

Running had been his main occupation recently. He was running from the people of Terra and from the Venusian beasts. The entire planet had conspired to destroy him.

Panting loudly he fell over the knee high root of a tree, rolled over his shoulder like a parachute jumper and turned around to face the creature. The root offered enough security as long as the threat came only from one side.

He squinted upward but the trunk of the tree was too smooth. It was 30 feet up to the first branches, making it impossible for him to climb up. The beast approached rapidly. With its length of more than 300 feet not even the highest tree on Venus could have offered a safe refuge.

Out of the underbrush slid the long pointed head of a slimy worm. It weaved left and right six feet above the ground. Failing to recognize any danger it advanced steadily.

When Marshall had first encountered the ugly creature about an hour ago, he had reached in desperation for his automatic rifle. The fear that the shots might betray him to his human pursuers was greater than his horror of the Venusian monster. He knew that the slimy giant worm possessed very limited intelligence and that it was highly dangerous because of its instinctive reactions. A victim fallen in its grip could only say his last prayer.

Against this seemingly boundless mass of repulsive flesh an attack with a conventional automatic gun was almost ineffective. After the first shock of surprise, therefore, Marshall took his thermo-impulse beamer and fired continuously for 20 seconds at the white body of the serpent. The result was only a division of the beast into two parts, both taking up the chase after him. The flight had cost Marshall his last energy.

Now he was lying behind the tree root which curved like a protective wall before him.

What if he aimed at the monstrosity in his gunsight squarely from the front?

It was only an idea which, however, nobody had tried out yet. The attack from the side had severed the body of the snake. How about a frontal approach? It would penetrate the body head on and, by concentrating the focus, the whole slimy body would be dissolved by the energy radiating from controlled nuclear fusion.

This was the way he had figured. He had no strength left to escape by running away. But he was still able to aim his weapon and pull the trigger.

The telepath John Marshall levelled his impulse-beamer. The top of the root presented a good support for accurate aiming.

His plan simply had to succeed because it was beyond his comprehension that he could die here away from human civilization and alone without witnesses.

The head of the huge worm swayed in front of his

gunsight. But it was not yet in the right position for his shot as the sinuous body still formed an angle with the axis of his impulse-beamer's bore.

When the distance to the loathsome worm had shrunk to 20 yards, Marshall suddenly realized that it had apparently changed its mind. Of course it was stretching the point a little to speak of a mind in view of the low capacity of the creature's brain, which contained nothing worth calling reason. It reacted strictly with reflexes to stimulations. This was Marshall's explanation for the senseless action of the worm.

It crawled toward the tree but passed it on the opposite side of the six foot trunk and continued sticking to a straight line in the direction of the undergrowth not far behind.

John Marshall held his breath. Not only his excitement but also the penetrating odour, to which no man from Terra was accustomed, forced him to choke. It took more than 15 minutes for the worm to go by. Nauseated and tantalized he finally sighed with relief when the tail of the monster disappeared harmlessly in the jungle.

Somewhere the worm would find a deep hole teeming with centipedes where it could crawl in and live in peaceful symbiosis with the scaly animals.

Marshall wiped the sweat from his brow. The sight of the white tail end of the worm aroused his curiosity. An hour ago, when he had cut the worm in two with his impulse beamer, both ends were burned black. Soon after a crust formed to seal them off and the other half of the worm grew a new head.

Marshall was aware of these strange peculiarities of

22

life on Venus and he knew that he was not yet out of danger.

It was his own fault that he had created two snakes out of one. And the reptile appeared just at the moment that he looked around to safeguard his position.

What had caused the first one to suddenly ignore him after it had hunted him stubbornly and methodically for an hour?

Marshall could think of only one reason. The movements of the fugitive had attracted its attention and prodded it continuously into his pursuit. When he threw himself behind the cover of the root and remained motionless, the goal had become unrecognizable for the primitive brain of the creature. The tactic of playing dead was valid for all worlds where the fight for existence took place according to eternal laws.

However, John Marshall was soon disappointed in his new hope.

Not that the second snake was smarter than the first one. But it just so happened by accident that it crawled exactly toward the root of the tree behind which Marshall was lying.

This time Marshall had to defend himself. He saw at the last moment that he would not get away by merely keeping watch. And the vehement move with which he jerked up his impulse beamer sufficed to draw the attention of the beast to him.

The white pointed snout shot forward. The first 15 or 20 feet of the serpent's length were on a straight line and the energy of the impulse beamer bored into the body.

His speculation was correct!

There was no partitioning and encasing in the lengthwise direction of the worm. Each of the transverse disks was a separate living unit. As soon as it was hit by the lethal energy it died away.

His success gave him new courage. With a last effort he dashed out from his hiding place and attacked. In a bloodthirsty frenzy he raced along the 50-yard-long creature and sprayed its white back with continued fire.

Then Marshall collapsed from exhaustion next to the mile-long slimy track. He had won but it resulted in utter helplessness for him. Even the pervading intolerable stench could not keep him from falling asleep on the spot.

The sun was still low in the east behind a milky veil of vapours when Marshall woke up again. His first glance fell on the chronometer. He had slept six hours Terrestrial time and he was still alive!

His nerves were calmer now and he was again in control of his limbs.

The six hours were spent like a child in innocent sleep. Children may have their guardian angels but Marshall could not put his trust for the future in celestial fantasies.

He looked at the sun in the east and checked the gyro-compass in his all-purpose wristband for his orientation. The flight from the worm had caused him to make a detour so that he was a few miles off. This deviation from his route was the least of his concerns. But it was essential that he reached the shore. It should be no more than 20 miles away. Considering that he had lost much of his strength this was quite a distance.

It meant that he would have spent three, four Terra days on the march. Maybe even a whole week or more.

He avoided mapping out the future in detail. The march through the wilderness had shattered much of his confidence. He was constantly plagued by hunger and thirst. He took a sip of his drinking water with the last bit of tea concentrate from his canteen. His breakfast consisted of half a pound of cold meat. After he had eaten it, he would have to go hunting again. But there was still time for that – till he got hungry again.

He licked the last bit of fat from his fingers and turned toward the east. The ocean was presumably somewhere in that direction. And somewhere in the west behind him, the patrols of Gen. Tomisenkov were roaming in search of him. To protect himself from them was evidently more important than warding off Venusian monsters.

The undergrowth was rather sparse in this environment. The ground was drier than in the lowlands. He encountered no particular trouble while covering the next miles. The visibility was not bad either. The breaking day with its uncertain future led him to take stock of his life. If one does not know what lies ahead and questions the wisdom of one's endeavors, it is best to recall how it all came about.

It was 10 years since John Marshall, the telepath of Perry Rhodan's Mutant Corps, had first set foot on Venus. At that time they had discovered far up in the northern hemisphere a mysterious fortress built by the humanoid Arkonides. It was constructed in the same period when men on Earth began to make use of the invention of the wheel, ventured cautiously in primitive boats out into the oceans and laid the groundwork for the Euclidian geometry to come.

During that era the Venus Arkonides, whose home was thousands of light-years away from the Solar system, were even said to have founded a colony on Earth. It later became extinct with the legendary Atlantis.

The second encounter between mankind and Arkonides took place in modern times. They met when the nuclear moon rocket under the command of the American, Maj. Perry Rhodan, discovered an Arkonide spaceship which had crashlanded on the backside of the moon. Only two of its crew still survived, the scientific leader Khrest, and Thora the commander. After Rhodan had established a politically neutral power in the Gobi desert with the aid of the superior Arkonide technology, the first expedition to Venus had lead to the discovery of the fortress in the north. The fully automatic positronic installation 'lived' by itself. The mighty robot brain conducted the defense of the Venus bulwark in accordance with the age-old programming until Rhodan first succeeded in aligning the positronic brain with his personal brain frequency so that it obeyed him now better than an Arkonide.

Years of progress on Earth and major expeditions in the interstellar reaches of the universe caused public interest in Venus and its fortress to somewhat wane.

But then political conspirators in the Eastern Bloc ignored their agreements with the New Power and provoked interminable entanglements. Concurrently, their spaceships invaded the Venusian planet in great numbers in order to subjugate it as a colony of the Eastern Bloc.

This attempt was not very successful. Whereas the political differences on Earth could be ironed out and a sound relationship restored, the conquest under Gen. Tomisenkov's leadership turned into a farce. He was unable to take over the positronic brain in the Venus fortress. The fuel carried in his spaceships was only sufficient for the one-way flight there. A second fleet with supplies and reinforcements had been decimated by Rhodan's intervention and barely reached Venus in ruins.

The invaders had become prisoners of Venus. The expedition disintegrated while living in the bush. Rebels split away from the main force remaining under the command of Gen. Tomisenkov. Illogical men like Lt. Wallerinski believed the time had come for another form of pacifism to be established by the brutal force of arms.

Marshall had frequently contemplated the strategic situation on Venus. However it was all a matter of conjecture. There was only one certainty, namely that Gen. Tomisenkov had forged the remnants of his troops into an effective striking force. He was the one Marshall had to reckon with, since his patrols were close on his heels. Twice already in the past days he had only narrowly escaped his pursuers.

Splinter groups like the pacifists under Lt. Wallerinski also constituted a danger. But only an accident could lead to a confrontation with them in the vast primeval forests and bushlands.

Of course the hazards to Perry Rhodan's crew were not limited to these eventualities.

Indeed it was only due to Thora's caprice that they

had become mired in this situation. Thora had for years longed only to return to faraway Arkon. As this had not yet met with Rhodan's approval, she had summarily high-jacked a Terrestrial spaceship to fly to Venus with a single robot to guard her. In her haste she had neglected to obtain the code signal so that the barrier on Venus had become insurmountable and her attempt was doomed. Rhodan didn't fare much better since his mind was exclusively set on her immediate pursuit.

Both of their ships foundered in the defense barrier of the bulwark extending 300 miles out. They crashed and found themselves in a situation no better than the invasion corps. Thora even fell into the hands of Gen. Tomisenkov, who held her captive. So far, Rhodan had not been able to liberate her. He had suffered a wound in the shoulder from a shot in a night skirmish that put him temporarily out of combat action. Even prolonged marches became too strenuous for him. As a result, only the limping mutant Son Okura stayed with him.

Marshall was sent on a special mission. It was a task that thrust him alone in the wilderness with the goal of reaching the shore of the ocean in the north.

He stopped walking. His physical weakness increased his perspiration and he used his handkerchief more frequently to wipe the sweat from his forehead.

What's the use? Why go on?

He stared longingly at his multi-purpose wristband containing among other gadgets an efficient radio transmitter. However, Rhodan had strictly ruled out the use of radio communications when there was a danger of listening in and being spotted.

His special mission tied in with an incident which happened years before. On the eastern shore of the two-hundred mile wide sea channel, Rhodan's men had previously encountered a semi-intelligent species of seals that proved to possess a very friendly nature.

After Rhodan's shoulder was injured, the march of 300 miles to the Venus fortress seemed to stretch into an eternity. Even if his wound healed quickly, it would remain a decisive handicap for the Chief of the New Power. One had to be very fit in order to stand up to the adversities of the Venusian wilderness.

Under these circumstances the recourse to the seals had been a very clever idea. If there was any help for them, the seals were their best hope of assistance. And if anyone could get in touch with the mammals, it was John Marshall, the telepath.

At 94:00 o'clock he reached the beach. When he stepped out of the thicket he paused in surprise. The sudden sight of the ocean gave him a feeling of suspicion since his unconscious mind had already given him the suggestion that he would never reach his destination. Then he broke into a run. The level shore was overgrown with knee-high reeds behind which a beach with clean yellow sand stretched to the water. Marshall finally stopped when the water lapped around his ankles.

The seals!

He began to concentrate. He expressed his desperate situation in his telepathic call for help. After a couple of minutes he relaxed again. His mind became passive and attuned to reception.

The impressions that closed in on him were frightening.

The apparently dead environment was in reality full of life. It hid in the reeds and in the water. And it was rife with thoughts; but they were entirely inhuman. They were far below the level of comprehensive intelligence; they were nothing but pure emotions. Instinctive reactions of a strictly primitive animal state. Nothing as precise as mathematical formula but permitting instead, various interpretations like an abstract painting. Nevertheless, Marshall believed he could understand the gist of the feelings. He could sense the lust, envy, hunger and ferocity emanating from the orchestra of emotions of the lowest creatures. But signals from the higher developed seals were entirely missing.

John Marshall was ready to abandon his concentrated effort in disappointment when a sign of alarm aroused his brain. All of a sudden a human thought crept into his receptive mind. It was a murderous thought originating from the coast.

He wanted to jump back and run away but he remembered in time that his life depended on keeping cool. The thought dwelled on killing and this intention was so clear that it revealed the choice of John Marshall as victim.

'This is the spy from the New Power, Rhodan's informer. You've evaded us for days. But you're here at the ocean and can't run away. You're going to be wiped out. You deserve no mercy. I ought to challenge you and let you look into the barrel of my weapon and watch my fire. But you're one of the

Rhodans. One of those with whom I can't take a chance.'

Marshall knew that the rifle was trained on his left shoulder. The man aimed for his heart. The minute he turned around the shot would be fired.

Instead, he threw himself into the water.

It was not deep enough to let his body submerge. But the reeds on the shore slightly shielded him.

The shot had gone off as he plunged down and it went wild above him.

The next thought at the rim of the forest was panic.

The killer was no longer able to see him and was thinking about flight. Marshall's reaction whipped up his superstition. Then fear of his superior and of the whole Venusian wilderness mingled in his mental struggle.

'I've got to kill him! If I don't get him, Tomisenkov will make my life miserable.'

John Marshall dragged himself through the foot deep water. Then he rolled onto the beach and crawled between the reeds, where he remained still and quiet.

'These Rhodans are sorcerers! The anxiety is driving me crazy. Only when all the Rhodans are dead, are we going to have peace. We've got to get rid of this nightmare. He must be killed!'

The thought-waves came closer – and with them the killer. He, too, had dropped to the ground and used the reeds as cover for his attack. He betrayed himself by the activity of his brain. He lifted his head above the rushes. Marshall knew the direction. All he had to do was to move the barrel of his weapon a hair to the left and pull the trigger.

When he got up and went over to his foe, he found only a corpse.

'Strange! They call us Rhodans although there's only one man with that name.'

Marshall knew that he was alone. He returned erect to the safety of the forest with a proud smile on his lips. He, too, was a 'Rhodan' in the vocabulary of the enemy.

'WORSE THAN PIRATES'

Gen. Tomisenkov had shifted his headquarters 30 miles to the east. It was situated on a high plateau with a sparse growth of trees overlooking the surrounding woods. In this manner he was in a favourable position to repulse any assault by the deserted rebel groups. He could have hidden his soldiers better in the forest but it was not his foremost concern to remain undetected. Everyone knew that he was in the area and they also knew that his troops outnumbered his adversaries. With such superiority he was not afraid of open confrontations.

Small tents and plastic shelters were pitched between the bushes growing no higher than the size of a man. The camp was cordoned off by a tight chain of guards.

Every six hours new passwords were issued to keep the rebels from smuggling into the compound. The patrol stalking the telepath consisted of only 12 men and was not required to use the password as Tomisenkov knew all of them personally.

Sgt. Kolzow saw a white piece of cloth appear suddenly from the ground.

'Password!'

'Lt. Tanjew of the shock troops. I must speak to the General.'

'Hands up! You may pass!'

A man jumped up and approached with raised arms.

'All right, Lieutenant. Go to the round bush over there. The General's tent is behind on the left. Anything new?'

'I didn't hear your last question, Kolzow. I have to talk to the General, not to you.'

Lt. Tanjew made the impression of a good soldier who had been in action for days without interruption, which was, indeed, the fact. He was at once admitted to Tomisenkov and saluted smartly.

'My men are holding up pretty well,' Tomisenkov thought with satisfaction. He greeted Tanjew with a smile that didn't reveal his curiosity. 'So you're still alive, Lieutenant. What do you have to tell me?'

'One of their men has reached the shore, sir!'

'Who?'

'As you know, sir, a battle has taken place south of the mesa between the rebels four days ago. We've determined that at least three members of the New Power were involved in that clash.'

'I know, Lieutenant!' Tomisenkov interrupted. 'I thought you were going to bring me news.'

'One of those men started to march alone to the east and we followed him according to your orders.'

'You were supposed to kill him or take him prisoner. What happened?'

Lt. Tanjew hesitated. 'We've not yet succeeded in catching him, sir. It's not easy to catch a single man when he's been warned.'

'Who could have warned him? There are hardly any people on Venus.'

'Private Lwow made a mistake. He rushed ahead on

34

his own. I don't like to place the blame on a dead man but ...'

'Lwow is dead?'

'Yes, sir! We found his body on the shore.'

'Then Rhodan's man was the better one again. Is it asking too much of you to execute such a simple operation with 12 men against one when you have all the strategical advantages?' The expression of benevolence had completely faded from Tomisenkov's face. 'Why did you come back, Lieutenant? To report your failure?'

'I'd like to request reinforcements, sir. We've come to the ocean and to be on the safe side we'll have to patrol at least five or six miles along the coast. I deem it necessary that each team consist of no less than three men. We need greater numerical superiority because we always turn out to be lacking in strength.'

'What do you mean by this contradiction?'

Tanjew hemmed again.

'Sir, you know the rumours among the men ...'

'The fairy tale of the giant and sorcerer, eh?' Tomisenkov said bitingly. 'Are you serious about these fantasies from the comics? If your commandos are so naive and gullible, I'll replace your platoon with grownup men, Lieutenant.'

'As you wish, sir. We'll do our duty. However, I consider the reinforcements an absolute necessity.'

'Because of those five miles along the coast?'

'Yes, sir!' Tanjew replied respectfully.

'Very well, I'll let you have them.'

Tomisenkov wrote an order.

'Take this to Col. Popolzak and select the men you

want. Next time I see you, I expect to get a good report. Thank you!'

'Thank you, sir! One more question. Do we still have to observe radio silence? A radio message would be advisable in an emergency.'

'You may leave, Lieutenant. I'm the one who will decide that. The radio silence must be maintained. I've got my reasons for it.'

* * *

One hour later, Lt. Tanjew left the headquarters with 25 soldiers.

The general didn't wish to be disturbed during that time. Tanjew's implications had given him food for thought, though he was loath to admit it openly. By the same token he had often felt intuitively that there was some truth to the wide spread rumours. There was nothing tangible about them, just wonderment about the success of Perry Rhodan and the 10 years of New Power.

He thought about Thora, the captured Arkonide, and about her robot R-17 that did not leave her side.

He clenched his fist and pounded on the flimsy camp table till it broke. It did not help to alleviate his agitation.

He went to the entrance and called loudly outside. 'Col. Popolzak!'

The Colonel crawled out of a nearby tent.

'Come here, Colonel! I need five dependable men.'

'Yes, sir! I'll send them over at once.'

'Let me finish first! I don't want to see the men.

Nobody must see them. Later on, I'm going to take a little walk with our prisoner outside the camp.'

Tomisenkov explained a few more details and went over to the hut housing Thora and her robot. 'Hello, Miss Thora! May I come in?'

'Oh, it's you, General! Since when do you practice such politeness?'

She stepped out of the hut and tossed her long flowing white hair back with a defiant gesture. Tomisenkov avoided meeting the cynical look of her slightly reddish eyes. Such duels with this woman had always irritated him.

'I'd like to invite you for a walk, ma'am. I'm sure you'll enjoy this beautiful morning on Venus.'

'I don't mind,' Thora quickly agreed, to his amazement. 'I'm sure you have another bag full of interesting topics in store for me. You always while away my time so pleasantly.'

Tomisenkov knew only too well that the Arkonide woman never cared much for his conversation. What he had up his sleeve today was even more disagreeable. The thought made him gloat and buoyed his spirit. 'Let me surprise you, ma'am!'

'I'm convinced you'll manage to do that. Take for instance that gun on your back.'

Tomisenkov had shouldered a rifle.

'You never know when you may get into unsafe territory. Being an expert on Venus, I won't have to explain to you how dangerous some of the animals are.'

'I should think it sufficient if we take R-17 along.'

'R-17 may be enough to protect you but I'm sure he wouldn't move a finger to save my neck. You'll have to leave it to me how to take care of myself on Venus.'

The guard posted at the exit of the camp saluted as the General and Thora and her robot passed.

'Why are you going so far outside?' Thora suddenly asked. Had she become suspicious?

Tomisenkov managed a smile.

'Don't worry, ma'am. We'll remain within shooting range of our headquarters. If you should entertain any thought of fleeing with your artificial friend, you better be warned. I have to talk to you privately.'

'We could have done that in your tent.'

'Let me be the judge of that! Please, be sure to tell me the truth – for your own good.'

'Is this supposed to be a threat?'

'You may always feel threatened if you cross me! Tell me something about your mutants.'

'What about them?'

'I'm referring to those mysterious people the world's press has been writing so much nonsense about for years. There must be some truth to it. Even Rhodan has hardly a chance in the jungle without his superior technical paraphernalia. Before he reaches the fortress in the north, his body will rot in the swamps.'

'But you believe that mutants are helping him? Let's assume that such is the case. Wouldn't his advantage be overwhelming without technical means? Besides, you're suffering from a delusion if you still believe that Rhodan has come to Venus with me.'

'Rhodan is here!' Tomisenkov said flatly. 'You might as well admit it.'

'I've told you the truth. What can I add to that? Evidently you know more about his whereabouts than

I. If he's still on Terra, it won't take more than a day on Venus till he comes to my rescue.'

'Before the day is out, we'll have reached the mountain up north. As soon as we take over the fortress, the whole planet will be in my control. If you're making secret plans to oppose me, it will be your loss, ma'am. On the other hand, if you throw in your lot with me, you may lead your life to suit yourself. The alternative is that you'll remain my prisoner forever. I've got the means to make life unpleasant for you, believe me!'

'I wouldn't doubt that in the least. Whenever you tell me something disagreeable you're always in character. Let's go back. This conversation is quite senseless.'

'What about the mutants?'

'We've got some on Arkon,' Thora answered. 'There are those who can read your thoughts and others who can influence them. The so-called teleporters simply "think" themselves from one place to another. They are always where they want to be. If I were a teleporter, for instance, I could be in the Venus fortress within two seconds.'

'Is Rhodan a mutant?'

'Not that I know. What makes you think so?'

'I've sent commandos out after him several days ago. They're breathing down his neck. Rhodan has reached the big north bay and is caught in a trap. Let's say he's no mutant, then I can expect to get my hands on him in a couple of Terra days.'

Thora didn't let on how badly Tomisenkov's information affected her. Although she had run away from Rhodan on Earth, she couldn't think of a more

39

welcome liberator. After the unforeseen crash in the Venusian jungle she came to regret her impetuosity.

'If you believe that it is Rhodan who has intruded into the north sea, why don't you get him? I can't prevent your doing it.'

Suddenly a shot rang out nearby. At the same moment a whistling bullet ricocheted from a rock.

'Take cover!' the General shouted but he ran at least 20 yards before he hit the ground. Thora had thrown herself down at once. However, the robot remained upright and sent a short burst of energy into the nearby woods, setting it on fire.

This was followed by a salvo of small arms fire.

It was obvious that the attack was directed solely against the Arkonide woman, since the fire was concentrated on her cover.

Simultaneously, the robot jumped to the fore.

Nobody would have suspected that R-17 could act with so much agility. A mantle shimmered around his body, looking like heated air.

Tomisenkov wondered whether it could be an energy screen. But he disregarded it and put a huge shell resembling a rifle grenade on the muzzle of his gun.

Meanwhile R-17 had taken up his position and sprayed the rim of the forest with uninterrupted energy fire. Soon the shooting from the conventional arms ceased. At this moment the general had sighted his aim. He pulled the trigger. Against the atomic rifle grenade the protection of the robot's energy screen proved to be ineffective.

R-17 went up in a short lived glowing cloud.

Seconds later, Tomisenkov was at Thora's side.

'I hope you didn't get hurt, ma'am! May I help you?'

Thora became only more confused by the manner in which the General approached her. She was unable to conceal her shock. R-17 had kept up her morale during her captivity and represented a certain measure of assurance. The attack looked very real but when she heard Tomisenkov's words she realized that she had been the victim of his intrigue.

She ignored his helping hand and got up by herself. 'What a miserable specimen of a *man* you are!' she flared.

Thora was wild with rage. Tomisenkov savoured his triumph all the more, even though unaware that the word 'man' from the mouth of this alien female woman was supposed to be the worst of insults.

'Let's return now, ma'am. I can imagine how much the loss of your plastic robot must upset you. I suppose you won't feel like continuing our little walk. You ought to lie down and take a little rest.'

'You'll pay for this, Gen. Tomisenkov!'

'Why?'

'Are you trying to deny that this contemptible manoeuver was your own handiwork?'

'Of course not. I give you credit for having found me out so quickly. Why can't you be a good loser, ma'am?'

Thora spat at his feet. She had seen some people do this and didn't care that it wasn't ladylike. Anyway, she disdained behaving according to the rules of human society. She knew no bounds when she was angry.

By now Tomisenkov knew his prisoner long enough to realize that there was no use talking to her in such a state. He silently turned around and went back to the camp. Thora passed by the guard 100 yards behind him. A soldier followed her at a distance to make sure she returned to her tent.

In the meantime the general had summoned the emergency detail to fight the forest fire. Although there were only small amounts of dry extinguisher chemicals left in storage, they were sufficient to put out the blaze. The succulent flora of Venus didn't make very good fuel. The weather on the planet lacked long periods of drought during which the prairies and forests could have become parched.

Tomisenkov's stubborness was proverbial. He went once more to Thora and inquired about the mutants.

'Get out of here, you barbarian!' she shouted at him and took a breath to heap some more invectives on him but words failed her when she saw his grinning face and she turned away quietly.

The General took a different tack and asked in a gentle tone:

'You once threatened that R-17 was capable of destroying all my troops and I took you seriously. Do you want to claim now that it was a harmless bluff?'

Thora didn't answer.

'Well, as you wish,' Tomisenkov grumbled. 'Don't take it for granted that I'm always ready to justify my actions to you. You threatened me with the robot and I didn't make a secret of it that I considered him a menace. I was the quicker one and now I have more power over you than before. You have two hours to rest up. Then we'll pull up stakes and depart for the north. The Venus fortress will be conquered, you can depend on that! And it will be I alone who will take possession of your ancestors' heritage. With you or without you.'

He received no reply and left, shrugging his shoulders.

When he passed the quarters of the shock troop near the central square he looked at the bulletin board. Popolzak had fastened on a new note with the names of the five men fallen in combat with R-17.

Tomisenkov suppressed a question about the sense of the action. He had a headache when he entered his tent.

* * *

Five hours later his little army was on the march again. The lower gravity of Venus made it easier for the men to carry the precious equipment and provisions salvaged from their disabled spaceships. It was not much considering what they were going to need in the next few months. For that reason they were forced to be very miserly with their few possessions. If anything was left behind because of carelessness or laziness, the culprit had to answer for it. Tomisenkov's orders were very strict in this respect.

All inventory of their stocks had been made several months ago. Since then inspections and checkups followed regularly at short intervals. Each match and bullet, each can of food was registered. Anyone firing a shot from his weapon had to keep a record and make a report.

The leading units and the rearguard were less loaded down with packs. They were the most mobile units. Each time Tomisenkov's troop completed another leg of the lengthy march and advanced their headquarters one more step northeast, he asked himself whether his optimism was justified in view of the dwindling strength of his army.

It was impossible to keep the column together in the marshes of the lowlands. The undergrowth was so dense that it had to be cleared with atom grenades. The atom grenades they used created 'clean' explosions without detrimental fallout. However, their application was limited by the danger of forest fires since their dry extinguishers were in very short supply.

The path broken by the vanguard had to be followed by all soldiers. The column, therefore, frequently extended over a distance of many miles.

With all these drawbacks Tomisenkov didn't have much to be proud of. He had approximately half a regiment left. The flanks were always exposed to an ambush even by a weaker enemy. And it was hardly appropriate to call a foe like Rhodan weak.

For that reason Tomisenkov always stuck close to Thora. He did it with such perseverance that Thora finally found her tongue again. She made it very clear to him that she didn't appreciate his company.

'I'm sorry I have to disregard your feelings. In case Rhodan attacks, I'll need a hostage. If he harbors any thought of rescuing you from here, I'll have the option of killing you first.'

His frankness astonished Thora. She took refuge in her inborn arrogance.

It was 113:00 o'clock when a member of the vanguard picked up a familiar rapid fire carbine. A sergeant brought the weapon to the general and reported:

'We've come across a campfire about two miles south of here, sir!'

'A campfire?'

'It was abandoned, sir. The burned wood was already cold. This carbine was lying in the grass under a tree. Those men must have forgotten to take it along. Some of our compatriots! It's a shame how derelict they become without a guiding hand.'

'Are you in charge of the vanguard?'

'Yes, sir!'

'Go to Col. Popolzak and have him give you 10 men. Take these reinforcements and reconnoitre in the southern direction. I've a feeling there must be some people there who need to be watched.'

'Very good, sir!'

Before the sergeant could reach the Colonel, who was marching 50 yards ahead, a volley of shots cracked out of the jungle.

'Take cover!' a voice cried. However the order was quite superfluous. Instinctively the men had hit the ground and turned right. While dropping to the ground their rifles were instantly moved into firing position.

All was quiet again after the first fire of the surprise attack. Even the singing Venusian birds in the trees interrupted their concert. Some flew away with flapping wings. Others stuck their heads under their feathers.

A few shots were fired from their own ranks.

'Hell, no!' Popolzak's voice could be heard distinctly. 'You're not allowed to fire unless you can see what you're shooting at. Every shot must be a hit!'

The unknown opponent answered with a burst of machinegun fire.

'The stupid idiots over there!' growled Tomisenkov, his nose half an inch above the ground. 'Don't they know they can't hit a man at 20 paces in this dense underbrush? This growth absorbs bullets like blotting paper ... Oh, I beg your pardon, ma'am!'

Tomisenkov had not noticed till then that he was pushing Thora into the ground. While he held the butt of his rapid fire gun in one hand his other gripped Thora's neck in a vice.

'If I hurt you, it was done unintentionally. You're much too valuable for me to lose you now. I won't permit the insurgents over there to decide when I let you die. They are worse than pirates. Is there anything I can do for you?'

'Let go of me and give me a weapon. I can handle it.'

'I don't doubt it,' Tomisenkov said tersely and reluctantly pulled out a sixshooter from behind his back. He handed it to Thora and said:

'Be careful, ma'am! It's loaded and suitable for close combat only.'

'That's good enough for me,' Thora declared with a vague look in her eyes.

4 'THE POWER IN HIS EYES'

Son Okura, the limping 'ultra-frequency seer,' and Perry Rhodan, the injured chief of the New Power, were not the most ideal team for a foot march on Venus. Their goal was 300 miles away, by direct flight, with a 200 miles wide sea channel in between, which also had to be crossed some time.

Son Okura's handicap had to be reckoned with from the beginning; but Rhodan's shoulder wound was a complication which was later acquired when both of them and John Marshall got involved in a fight with the rebels and Lt. Wallerinski's 'pacifists.' However, Perry had not lost his sense of humor. A shot went through his flesh close to the armpit. No bone or important muscle was damaged but Rhodan was still reminded by repeated itching and jabbing pains that his freedom of action was restricted.

'You've got to take care of yourself, sir,' Okura kept admonishing him. He had built another tree house of vines and broad leaves. It was perfectly camouflaged.

'Your tree houses are for people who enjoy luxury and comfort,' Rhodan chided him, 'not for people who want to get ahead.'

'We've agreed, sir, that security comes first. Besides, we've got no other choice with our handicaps.'

'I'm not so sure we're not taking part in a race. We don't have a guarantee that Tomisenkov and Thora can't enter the bulwark in the mountain if they reach it first. Thora is an Arkonide whose brain will be recognized.'

'Do you believe she'd betray us?'

'You can't call it betrayal. She's in the hands of an enemy who can force her.'

'Okay,' Okura smiled. 'I'm convinced that we can beat Tomisenkov in a race. Despite the slow progress we're making, we're faster than he is. Tomisenkov simply can't haul his army as quickly through the jungle as we can drag our invalid bodies. After the search I made yesterday, I'm certain that the remnant of Tomisenkov's division is not far from here. We've almost caught up with him and I believe we'll get to the coast before he does. There's no need to worry about Marshall.'

'I wish I could share your confidence,' Perry Rhodan replied. 'You've got to think in strategic as well as in tactical terms. Don't forget to consider the picture as a whole.'

'I don't understand you, sir.'

'So far we've only dealt with the people we've encountered in the immediate neighbourhood. Let's start from the beginning and find the reason for the present situation.'

'The reason for our presence here is Thora's flight.'

'Right! Now think about the other Earthmen!'

'The Eastern Bloc has sent Tomisenkov with a division to invade Venus and we've thrown a monkey wrench into that expedition. His army is almost destroyed. Apparently he still commands a small remnant of it . . .'

'Go on! Forget about the deserters. There must be many more men on Venus.'

Son Okura paused to think.

'From the Eastern Block?'

Perry Rhodan nodded.

'Of course, my boy!'

'You've the relief armada in mind. No, sir. I've already given this some thought. Remember when we first met Sgt. Rabow, who died in the battle with the rebels and the pacifists? He has told us many things but he never mentioned that the second fleet has landed.'

'That's just it. Tomisenkov evidently doesn't know anything about it either. But there's no doubt in my mind that the fleet has landed. I told you that you must always start from the beginning. The Eastern Bloc has launched 200 spaceships. We've destroyed 34 of them when we accidentally passed through the core of their vessels with our energy screen around us. Perhaps more ships were smashed up during the landing; but I'm willing to bet that more than 100 ships have arrived intact on Venus.'

Son Okura paled. 'My god, sir! This would mean . . .'

He didn't have to finish his sentence. They both knew the importance of the fact that somewhere on Venus an army with excellent equipment existed.

'It's obvious that the armada was meant to reinforce Gen. Tomisenkov's troops. The fact that nobody has reported to him proves they've mutineered, too. Mutiny seems to be epidemic on Venus,' Rhodan declared dryly.

They didn't talk much more about the subject although it was of the greatest interest to them. Their schedule now required six hours of rest. It was more important to recuperate and conserve their strength than to speculate about strategy. There was plenty of time for that during the march.

*　　*　　*

They slept and departed according to their time plan. Okura had lost count of the tree houses he had built in the Venusian forest. He had become quite an artist. Each drawing was more beautiful than the last one. Yet they had to leave them without ever seeing them again.

They talked about such little sentimentalities when they tired of discussing the serious problems. The conversation usually ceased entirely after a few miles on the march when it was again brought home to them that the wilderness on Venus demanded continuous toil.

On the following day – for convenience sake they usually counted the days on the Terranian calendar – they heard some shots. Rhodan, who was walking ahead at the moment, immediately stood stock still. Before he could say anything another volley followed.

'There seems to be a battle due north of here, sir.'

'Where else? That's where Tomisenkov hangs out.'

They heard one more detonation of a bomb or grenade. Then it was silent. They waited 15 minutes but there was no more shooting.

'H'm, what do you make of it, Son?'

'They probably are in a military encampment. From

a hedgehog position they can easily repulse Wallerinski's raids.'

'If it was Wallerinski!'

They continued to surmise several possibilities without getting at the truth. They did not know that Gen. Tomisenkov had destroyed robot R-17.

'We want to keep a little more to the left,' Rhodan decided. 'Our distance from the Easterners is much too great. Caution can be overdone, too.'

'One can never be too careful,' Okura opined. His boss smiled at the lecture.

'Of course not. Still, there's a possibility that we're needed. By Thora, for instance.'

Rhodan's plan was put in operation. After six more miles they built another tree house and made themselves comfortable. Before going to sleep they made their usual attempt to establish radio communications with Bell. They pulled the tiny pin of the antenna out and kept calling persistently. However, *Good Hope V* failed to answer. There was the same silence as on all the previous days.

'Secret barrier X,' Rhodan murmured. 'It really seems to be in effect.'

'Or Bell has already long ago returned to Earth.'

'He promised to stick around. Be that as it may, from now on we're strictly on our own. Good night, Son!'

'Good night, sir!'

It sounded incongruous as the morning sun was still high in the Venusian sky.

This time they were awakened from their sleep by the explosions of firearms. Okura felt Rhodan's warning hand on his arm. 'Quiet, my boy! It must be quite close.'

Indeed, it sounded as if the firing came from below their tree. However, the foliated crowns of the 50 yard high trees distorted the acoustics.

They peered through the leaves of their hut.

'I can't see a thing,' Okura said.

'No wonder, with this obstructed view,' Rhodan grunted. 'If I only knew ... What the devil is going on there?'

He pointed to a spot where his companion also recognized some movement. There were people in the underbush, no more than 100 yards away.

More shots rang out. The gun fire, at first staccato, was followed by a hail of shots.

'The battle is farther left. Probably 500 yards from here. But obviously some men are moving around down there.'

'Right, sir! I saw someone's head.'

'Okay. I'm going to take a look.'

'I wouldn't do that, sir. They'll ...'

Rhodan waved him away.

'They'll do nothing because I'll be careful. You stay here and hold the position. Whatever happens, don't give yourself away by shooting. Most likely a group of rebels is stationed there. Perhaps they've got something to eat for us. We've got to have more ammunition and food.'

Son Okura was accustomed to following orders. He merely nodded silently.

Rhodan slipped over the edge of the platform. If he descended slowly enough, the risk of discovery was remote. The dense foliage and parasitic lianas provided good cover all the way down to the ground.

He had to lower himself about 20 yards. To relieve his right shoulder he put his weight on his left hand.

He reached the ground undetected. Visibility was now even more limited. He knew the direction and worked his way forward. The continuing fight distracted the foreigners. None of the rebels even suspected that someone was behind their backs. There was more of a danger from Venusian animals than from deserted soldiers but Rhodan had learned from experience to watch his surroundings.

Rhodan was in luck. He evaded caterpillars, bugs and swarming butterflies. They could be poisonous but they left him alone. Any attack by them could have occurred only by happenstance.

The vines were a more difficult obstacle. At times they formed tight hedges so that he was compelled to squeeze himself through like a snake. To cut these tough plants would have taken too much time. Moreover, there was always the danger that they were under tension. Rhodan had often observed how the severed lianas whipped like a bowstring. They made a noise that aroused suspicion and they could kill a man if he had the misfortune to be hit by one of them.

When no more than 30 yards separated him from the camp, he paused for a while. His hands and face were scratched up. He wiped the sweat from his eyes with a handkerchief and noticed that it was stained with blood.

Minor scratches and abrasions, thought Rhodan as he contemplated the discovery behind which lurked the disquieting doubt whether it was wise to minimize the hazards of the unknown wilderness of this planet. To be sure, botanists had studied the Venusian flora but only a small part had been classified and chemically analyzed. Each innocuous looking thorn could carry deadly germs.

Rhodan rid himself of this distressing thought with determination and concentrated on the people in front of him. He had no trouble listening in on their conversation. They were rather taciturn and all he could learn was that they were tired and thought that Wallerinski's attack on Tomisenkov was too perilous. They spoke in such low voices that Rhodan was unable to hear all their words.

He would have to get a little closer.

Moving cautiously, he advanced much slower than before. The battle in the distance had grown fiercer and there was little probability that the rebels would return very soon. Unless, of course, Wallerinski suffered a decisive defeat and was overrun by Tomisenkov's troops.

Finally, Rhodan discovered a small clearing. Just a place where the grass was trampled down. Its diameter was 20 yards at the most. The interlocking treetops formed a dense roof above and permitted no more light to reach the ground than elsewhere. The orchid-like blossoms of the vines displayed their gorgeous colours in the murky twilight.

Rhodan saw five men.

Four of them were sleeping or just lying in the grass. The other sat leaning against a tree.

The equipment guarded by the soldiers made Rhodan envious. In particular, they were well provided with handguns. In addition to several boxes with descriptive labels at least 40 or 50 automatic carbines were lying under a tree close to him.

'The president ought to clarify his ideology,' one of those lying in the grass said. 'It's not a very original idea to fight for peace with force.'

'You mean we can be real pacifists only when everybody else is a pacifist.'

'Nonsense! We're already true pacifists. You must be sleeping in class.'

The man against the tree made an exasperated gesture.

'Quit your ignorant babbling. All that matters now is what the president will accomplish. This engagement already lasts much too long for my taste. If an ambush doesn't come off at once, I can see nothing but trouble.'

'You're going to be in trouble the way you're shooting off your mouth, Igor. The president knows what he's doing. I've got complete confidence in him.'

'He'll be very proud of that, Mitja. I also know that he thinks you're a smart aleck. He doesn't like people like that.'

'Think what you want. I know he likes me; that's all I care. If you're referring to the advice I gave him, I can assure you that Wallerinski was very grateful. We'll set that trap from the trees as soon as we reach the river.'

'Oh no! You've really talked him into that? Then why did he attack the General today?'

'Why don't you ask him yourself? At any rate, I

know enough about tactics that such a ruse would merely be a game of hit or miss in this neighbourhood. But Tomisenkov must ford the river above the cataracts. There's no better place to cross the river within miles. Remember that there's an opening like a path in the forest on the other side of the river. Tomisenkov will simply have to pass through there if he wants to get to the ocean. All we have to do is to sit in the trees ...'

'When are you going to shut up?' a third man complained. 'The way you're trying to outshout each other, Tomisenkov's patrols will be here before our own men. You're supposed to stand guard, Mitja! Keep your eyes and ears open! The others, get down. If it doesn't suit you, you can tell it to the president; but don't give me any trouble!'

The last speaker appeared to be a sort of sub-lieutenant. In any case, he was in charge. Perry Rhodan would have preferred that the men kept talking. It had distracted them and now the slightest noise could betray him.

He was compelled to use the background noises of the forest's inhabitants so that his advance would not be heard. If he waited for the sound of flapping wings or the call of a bird, he was able to move forward without being detected. It slowed down his progress more than he anticipated.

He fashioned a loop from a finger-sized vine and pushed it little by little over the barrel of a carbine. He jerked the loop so that it snagged behind the front sight. It took an eternity till he finally gained possession of the weapon. However, he still lacked ammunition and food.

As his next objective he selected a small box labelled 'Meat Extract.' He made the loop a little larger and managed to slide it over the box; but when he pulled the sling, the box toppled over, alarming the guard instantaneously. 'Halt!' he commanded although it was impossible for him to see Rhodan. At the same time the other four jumped up and grabbed their weapons in a routine manner.

Rhodan realized instantly that he had no chance of escaping from this battery of drawn guns. He could only compensate for their numerical advantage by using his head and bluffing them.

He just stood there nonchalantly, without raising his new found weapon.

'Put your hands up!' he was challenged.

He paid no attention, stepped over a root of a tree lying in his way and approached the five soldiers, pretending to be annoyed.

'Don't move!'

Rhodan complied. Though he was amused, he did it with the expression of a disapproving superior officer.

'Who is in charge here?' he asked in a commanding tone.

His authoritative bearing evidently confused the five soldiers. They no longer insisted that he put up his hands.

'Hell, can't you talk?' Rhodan thundered, playing the role. 'What's the shooting over there all about? Do you know who's playing war there?'

Finally one of the men managed to speak.

'My name is Ilja Iljushin, sir!'

'You've got a rank, haven't you?'

'All ranks have been abolished since President Wallerinski ...'

'Shut up!'

Perry Rhodan's voice grew louder and louder, since he saw that his imperious behaviour created the desired effect.

'For your information, I'm Commissar Danow, R. O. Danow. There's been a change of government in the Eastern Bloc four weeks ago. The new government has dispatched strong forces to Venus which landed yesterday to restore law and order. I get the impression from our short talk that some strange customs have developed in Tomisenkov's division which will hardly meet with the approval of the government. I advise you to remember your oath of loyalty and to return to your duties.'

'We don't serve under Tomisenkov, Commissar ...'

Rhodan saw that Mitja poked the speaker in the ribs. However it was too late to deny the admitted mutiny.

'We'll talk about the details later. First of all you must see to it that this silly shooting match stops. What did you say the name was – Wallerinski?'

'Lt. Wallerinski, Commissar!'

'You two will leave at once and inform him about the new situation. The power of command has been exclusively assumed by the appointed commissars. I expect to see Lt. Wallerinski and his detachment here in half an hour latest. What are you waiting for?'

Rhodan had looked instinctively at the two 'pacifists' he considered more independent. He had to get rid of them for a short time. They obeyed.

After they had disappeared toward the north in the underbrush, he had only three opponents to contend with. The improvement of the odds in his favour made him feel more optimistic.

'Lay down your arms! I can't permit you to bear arms until you've renewed your oath.'

For a few moments it looked as if he had gone too far and that his bluff would be called by the three 'pacifists.' The men hesitated. Without their becoming aware of it, Rhodan then resorted to a different treatment.

He still kept his weapon lowered. It would not have looked very well if he had tried to level the heavy carbine and dropped it. It was still too much of an effort for his injured shoulder.

His eyes, though had not suffered. The power of his eyes could not be explained by common hypnosis. It was one of the by-products of his Arkonide hypnotraining.

The hesitation of the soldiers was fraught with danger.

'Put down your arms!' he ordered once more.

He said it without adopting the barking tone of a drill sergeant. He hardly raised his voice but it did not fail to be persuasive.

The pacifists obeyed.

'Detachment, about face!'

The command was crisp as on a parade ground.

Once again the astounded men followed the order.

Rhodan picked up their weapons and threw them behind his back with the exception of one light army pistol which he could securely hold in his hand in spite of the pain in his shoulder.

Then he made them turn around again and they were facing him eye to eye. This time the pistol gave him the edge. Even the next experiment succeeded although it would have been extremely difficult to perform with men indoctrinated to a lesser degree with blind obedience. For them Rhodan represented Commissar R. O. Danow. They did him the favour of tying each other up with thin but tough vines. Rhodan took care of the rest. He tied them to three trees with their faces facing north and – for the sake of added security – put gags in their mouths.

After their treatment the three 'pacifists' slowly began to realize that they had been tricked by a very clever ruse, albeit the knowledge came five minutes too late.

They continued to hear noises behind them indicating that their wily adversary was busy with their property. Finally they heard him walking away amidst the sound of moving vines.

*   *   *

When Perry Rhodan got back to his tree, he wanted to send up a signal but Son Okura was already beside him.

'I could hear you talk loudly, sir, and I guessed that you were detected. So I came down.'

'You'll have to climb up again and get our stuff. We've got to get out of here as quickly as possible. I'll explain later.'

The ultra-frequency seer was pleased to see the two carbines, the pistols and the sack full of canned food. Then he clambered up and brought down their few things.

'We'll have to move all this stuff as fast as possible,' Rhodan declared. 'In 20 minutes Wallerinski is going to find his three tied-up guards. If we don't have a good head start, we'll get into plenty of trouble.'

'I'll last a few miles,' the small Japanese said cheerfully and put more than half of the baggage on his back.

They were in a lower part of the forest where the growth was so dense that it looked as if some giant had knitted it together in an intricate pattern. A fast march was out of the question regardless of how hard they tried; but every step forward was a little more security gained. The primeval forest was growing so vigorously that it seemed to be – by human standards – in fast motion.

Reginald Bell once declared that it was actually possible to see the growth if one stared at it for two minutes. This was true in a sense. The path of Rhodan's and Okura's flight would be virtually unrecognizable by pursuers half a Terra-hour later.

*　　*　　*

'I'm out of ammunition,' Thora panted. She was close by the side of the general. He handed her two new clips.

'These are the last ones I've got. If they're gone you'll have to crawl back 200 yards and get some from

61

the supply depot providing it's still in our hands. Shoot only when you can see the enemy clearly.'

'If you say so, General!'

The engagement had already lasted well over 15 minutes. More than 30 men had crowded around Gen. Tomisenkov and formed a hedgehog position.

Not one of Wallerinski's pacifists had dared come closer than a stone's throw to their miniature fortress.

Tomisenkov's order to conserve ammunition was not only meant for Thora. He passed the instructions on down the line. 'Never fire unless you're sure to hit somebody. I can't pull bullets out of a hat.'

Nobody had any thought of abandoning their position. He had lost contact with the other members of his troop. However, the sound of uninterrupted rifle fire from several directions was proof that they had taken up similar defensive positions. Tomisenkov was convinced that Wallerinski was not in control of the battle. He had already twice heard the voice of the ambitious lieutenant breaking in anger as he shouted his orders.

'Listen to that, ma'am! The president is getting hoarse from yelling. The president! Get that? That young brat calls himself president! The entire planet is a lunatic asylum! Watch me – this is how you do it. I bet you haven't even noticed it. Over to the left of the three purple orchids is another dead body now, a "pacifist" who wanted to play war.' Tomisenkov ended his words with a gruesome laugh.

One hour later he was as hoarse as his rival. He was so irritated that he could barely whisper when he gave his commands.

Wallerinski had suddenly broken off the engagement. His orders were audible in Tomisenkov's position.

'This could be a feint,' the General told Thora. This suspicion was shared by all and so they waited a little. Then Tomisenkov sent messengers to the front and rear and directed his troops to close ranks. The officers were called for a consultation while the noncoms and privates collected their fallen comrades.

This was a painful task which delayed their march for many hours. Yet this was only one of their hardships.

'You'll have many heartbreaks on this planet,' Thora had told the General. Now he was reminded of her prediction.

They found over 50 bodies. More than half were Wallerinski's followers. However, their own losses were not all accounted for.

'We're short 27 men,' Tomisenkov stated at the review to the officers. 'What's your explanation, Colonel?'

Popolzak shrugged his shoulders indifferently.

'They must have overlooked a few bodies.'

'Not 27!'

'Some might have gone over to Wallerinski. How do you know on whose side your soldiers' sympathies are?'

'Col. Popolzak! What kind of loose talk is this? It seems to me you too have been infected by this planet.'

'We're all infected, General! Everybody is susceptible in some way. And you're no exception either.'

'And what exactly do you mean by that.'

'You're labouring under the delusion that you're

commanding disciplined troops when the fact is the men are in rags, they don't give a damn about discipline once they are out of earshot and curse you because of your inability to face the facts. Their herd instinct is the only reason you have this pitiful remnant of your airborne division left. Otherwise they would've run away long ago if they could. Wherever they turn, hell opens up. They stick together mainly because of fear and for self-preservation. Don't think that anyone believes you can lead them into paradise. Even your plans to conquer the Venus fortress are considered nothing but pipe-dreams and fairy tales.'

Deadly silence followed Popolzak's lengthy speech.

The General had turned white as a sheet and the devastating answer did not come. 'Is that true?' he finally asked softly and they all knew that it was not because he wanted to save his strained vocal chords.

There was no response. No one else dared state an opinion.

'Well,' Tomisenkov nodded after a pause, 'I'll think about what you've told me, Colonel. I suppose all of us are now much too upset to deal objectively with these matters.'

The column resumed its march.

At 143:00 o'clock they reached the river and crossed it at the ford above the waterfalls where the natural lane opened up in the forest, promising an easy walk.

At that point a sergeant brought a note one of his soldiers had found pinned on a tree. It read:

'Gen. Tomisenkov, do not take this path. The pacifists are hiding in the trees and plan to ambush you.'

'Who the devil, could have written this?' Tomisenkov wondered.

Thora could have told him where it came from since she recognized the handwriting. But she chose to remain silent.

5. RHODAN TO THE RESCUE

John Marshall felt he had reached the end of his rope.

Half a morning on Venus was more than a full day on Earth. During all that time he had tried to draw the attention of the seals.

He knew they inhabitated the shore on the opposite side of the sea channel. This distance was so far as to discourage even a born optimist. By the same token, the sea was the element of these semi-intelligent creatures. Was it not natural to assume that they swam far out and came close to the beach on this side?

Why didn't they hear him?

Had they followed a nomadic instinct and gone to another place? Yet other seals were bound to take their place if they had left. No biological vaccum ever persisted in the abundant life of Venus.

John Marshall went out to the farthest point. A mile and a half from the spot where he had reached the ocean a flat spit of land extended deep into the water. It was not much more than a sandbar. The grass cover ended after 100 yards. His footprints left a mile long track seemingly leading into a dead end of hopeless desolation.

He stood at the tip of the land ridge, surrounded by water on three sides. The ocean reached as far as the horizon. The hills in the north were far below the brim of the water.

It was all very depressing.

Why didn't the seals hear him?

The intensity of his telepathic luring grew weaker and weaker. He required longer pauses to recover his strength. It was not the physical fatigue alone which hindered his concentration but also the emotional depression he suffered.

Why didn't they hear him?

The constant question produced a shock as he suddenly seemed to have found the answer. Their frequencies were not attuned! Transmitter and receiver must be synchronized in conformance with the simple basic laws of physics. Marshall recalled his first encounter with the seals when they needed an array of technical instruments to establish communications between them and humans. The seals 'talked' with each other in the ultrasonic range and it was inaudible for human ears. The ultrasonic waves had to be transformed with the aid of a frequency-communicator and then the language of the seals was made comprehensible by using the cerebral analyzer and the positronic decoder.

Marshall was at first completely consternated. Then he realized that he had failed to think his problem through to the end. After all, Perry Rhodan was not such a half-wit as to send him out alone into the wilderness if the circumstances were utterly hopeless.

'I'm a good telepath,' he kept telling himself. 'I don't need these technical crutches. Thought waves are thought waves – of the same frequency! This is true for the seals as well as for me. They've got to hear me! Unless their apathy is to be blamed for ignoring my call for help.'

He stretched out on the sand to relax half an hour without moving a finger. He let his mind go blank.

After the time had elapsed, he dug a hole in the sand with his hands and put the few things he carried in it. The hole slowly filled up with water but his carbine and the cans of food were not affected by the moisture.

Unburdened by his pack, he walked out into the ocean, deep enough to submerge his whole body. He was aware of the gamble he took. The slimy water was flowing – unlike that of Terra – almost like oil because it was more saturated with algae, seaweed and miniscule life. It could hold many surprises beyond the scope of human research. But Marshall had no choice.

Water propagates soundwaves faster and more intensively than air. Perhaps it could do the same for the vibrations of a telepathic brain.

He submerged completely in the water and concentrated on a simple vocabulary to enable the seals to grasp his message.

Periodically he raised his head above the water to breathe.

He repeated this process five times. The last time a burst of fire from a machinegun spattered close to him and forced him to duck again very quickly.

This put an instantaneous end to his preoccupation with the seals. Behind him were people who represented a menace much greater than any throughout the mysterious world of Venus.

He groped his way under water to the right until his empty lungs compelled him to come up for air. In doing so he turned around on his back in order not to expose his whole head. Only his face showed above the water. Out of the corners of his eyes he caught sight of a group of six men walking out on the strip of land without making an effort to hide themselves. They seemed to know that they held the upper hand. Evidently they had watched Marshall for some time and observed that he left his weapons at the tip of the narrow shoal of sand. Perhaps they believed that they had already finished him off. At any rate, they had stopped shooting and simply approached at a rapid pace.

The rise of the sandbar was barely enough to keep Marshall out of sight when he pressed himself flat against the ground. It was clear that he could not remain another second in the water. If the enemy got to his cache before him, he had lost his last chance.

He continued swimming on his back until he touched bottom behind him. Then he rolled around on his belly and began to crawl forward.

When he had dug the hole for his cache, he had inadvertently thrown up a little pile of sand which could now save his life.

He crawled a little to the left till the excavated sand was exactly in the line of sight between him and the six men. Then he crawled forward again and reached his possessions without being detected.

The six men were still approximately 200 yards away.

He burrowed deeper into the sand and took out the

two weapons. One was a heavy automatic rifle he had captured and the other the handy impulse beamer of Arkonide origin. As soon as he felt the butt of the rifle against his shoulder his confidence returned.

He took a deep breath and aimed carefully.

The barrel rested on the pile of sand. At the last moment before pulling the trigger he raised the barrel just enough to fire over the heads of his attackers, since he intended to warn them first. More than fair!

Was it possible to be fair in a fight where the enemy gave no quarter?

Marshall didn't know but he didn't regret what he had done.

His opponents were startled. If they had turned around and run away, Marshall would never have thought of shooting them in the back. Instead the six took a different attitude. They dropped to the ground and went on the offensive.

A salvo of big calibre bullets hit around him and made the dirt fly up in the air. Marshall knew that his pile of sand offered little protection. He could no longer practice restraint if he cared to survive this trap.

These men were out to kill him. Their thoughts were very similar to those of the one he had had to fight off a few hours before.

Marshall put down the automatic rifle and trained the impulse beamer on the cover behind which the invisible foe was hiding.

Ten seconds of continuous bombardment with pure thermal energy! It was enough to make the snow burn and what chance did these people have in such a hell?

They were certain to be dead. Nevertheless, Marshall waited a full hour before he moved.

He had snuffed out the lives of seven men. However it was plain to see that the hostile detachment was by no means completely annihilated. Obviously, there were many more in the special team sent out to hunt him down. A company of soldiers could be hiding in the nearby forest.

His suspicion was soon confirmed. He heard another shot in the distance and could see two men running across a clearing and disappear in the underbrush.

The enemy had become more prudent after observing the demonstration of his raygun. It was unnecessary for them to take any chances. Marshall was caught in a trap. The 800 yard long outjut of land was connected to the shore by a very narrow stretch. If he tried to escape across this little strip, he would become an easy target for the hidden sharpshooters. To fire at random into the forest would have been the height of folly. Even his Arkonide impulse-beamer was simply nothing but a toy against the Venusian jungles.

John Marshall had no other choice than to build up his present position. Lying on his side, he dug out the sand with the butt of his rifle. He made himself a foxhole in which he could stretch out. The water seeping in had to be ignored.

The pile of sand was also reinforced, more in breadth than height. It had to have sufficient mass to absorb big calibre bullets. He couldn't even think of protecting himself against any heavier reinforcements his foes might bring up such as grenade rifles or pos-

71

sibly light cannons.

He had to be prepared for the worst.

If only the seals would show up! He needed some allies very desperately. But would they help one man against others? He trusted in that, given that he was a telepath.

However, his predominant hope rested on Perry Rhodan who was to follow him slowly with Son Okura. Where were they now?

Marshall fingered his wristband containing among other gadgets a micro-transmitter. Use of the radio was strictly prohibited. But Rhodan had also authorized the sending of an emergency message in the most urgent case. The decision was up to Marshall.

Would they consider him a coward if he called for help? He hesitated for a few minutes. Then he made up his mind and turned the little wheel which switched on the transmitter. He pulled the miniature antenna out with his fingernails. The wavelength had already been set.

'Calling Perry Rhodan! John Marshall speaking. Calling Perry Rhodan! This is an emergency, sir ...'

He waited 10 seconds.

The impulse from his transmitter automatically activated the receiver.

Then came the answer.

'This is Rhodan! What's wrong, Marshall?'

'The seals didn't come, sir. I'm afraid the distance is too great. I've tried for hours without success. The enemy is breathing down my neck. I've been surrounded on a strip of land without trees or grass and only a little pile of sand as cover. The enemy is waiting in the forest. I'm fairly safe from small arms but I must expect them to lob in rifle grenades. They're determined to get me. Can you do something to help me?'

'Damn it, John, you're in a hell of a mess. I'm glad you called me. Tomisenkov and the rebels are so busy clobbering each other right now that we don't have to worry about being intercepted by their radio detectors. Okura and I have managed to get ahead of the General's troops and we've already gained a good lead. I guess we can join you in about four hours. Try to hold out till then! Give us a short radio signal every 10 minutes so we don't lose our direction. Keep your chin up, Marshall! We'll get you out!'

Soon after finishing the call, the soldiers on the shore renewed their barrage. Marshall spotted the flashes from their muzzles in three places and answered their fire with his impulse-beamer.

Two thirds of the raygun's energy was still effective at 1000 yards. A bluish white light flashed at the rim of the forest and its heat caused the succulent vegetation to vaporize. In no time a strip along the shore was engulfed in man-made fog.

'Hey!' Marshall exulted. 'A bonus! I hadn't even thought of this effect. I'll keep it up and keep 'em in a fog. That ought to but 'em and keep them busy for a while.'

*   *   *

'Come on, Okura! We'll have to step on it, we two cripples. Can you make it?'

The frequency seer forced a valiant little grin.

73

Rhodan could see that the boy's strenuous effort had exceeded his strength.

'All right, Son! Let me have those three shooting irons and the bag with the food. It's my turn to be the pack burro.'

'Don't talk as if I'd carried everything up to now. You've got to take it easy with your shoulder.'

'Nonsense! My shoulder's getting much better. Give me the stuff and take the machete. You can go first the next few miles. That'll give you enough to do.'

The slender Japanese gave in and they penetrated deeper into the jungle.

They had crossed the river long ago.

Meanwhile Rhodan had received Marshall's call for help and it was now impossible for him to remain close to Thora. He was forced to reach the ocean as quickly as feasible. He could only hope that someone from Tomisenkov's troop had found his note, warning them about Wallerinski's planned ambush from the trees.

Hours had passed and they had not heard a shot.

'I'm certain they found the note,' Okura assured him. 'We couldn't have failed to notice the battle if Tomisenkov had passed under the trees and fallen into Wallerinski's trap.'

'I suppose Thora is safe for the time being. It won't take much longer till we get to her. When night comes, you'll be our biggest help, Son!'

Perry Rhodan was referring to Okura's gift as ultra-frequency seer. Although he required glasses for normal sight, his eyes had an ability unmatched by any other man. The range of his vision extended far into the wavelengths of ultra-violet and infra-red. He was, therefore, capable of seeing with perfect clarity at night.

'When night comes ...' Okura repeated and it sounded as though he longed for it. 'I can't help it, sir, but I prefer the change of night and day on Earth. There are still three days until night here. And we'll have to rescue Marshall from his precarious position in that time.'

'I'm afraid,' Rhodan replied, 'we won't have that much time left.'

Recently they had made comparatively good progress, not because the terrain had become less tortuous but rather because they had learned to improve their routine of travelling through the jungle.

At regular intervals they received Marshall's radio guide signals, enabling them to take the shortest way to him.

At about 152 : 00 o'clock Rhodan claimed he could smell the ocean.

'You'll have to be extremely careful now, Son,' Rhodan warned. 'The woods are full of fighters.'

Then they suddenly stood at the ocean. It had come into view without warning. Only a minute ago they had struggled through the thickest undergrowth obstructing their sight.

'Look at that fog!' Rhodan muttered. 'I can't see a thing.'

Okura smiled.

'It's a very peculiar fog, sir, but it doesn't disturb me. It's getting denser toward the left if I'm not mistaken.'

'No, you're right, Son. Can you recognize anything?'

'I can see right through it. At least 20 men are lying in the grass at the edge of the forest less than 300 yards from us. They seem to think they can use the fog as a cover.'

'And where's Marshall?'

'The landstrip begins a little farther back.'

'Now I can see the tip way out there. I recognize a black spot. That must be John. I don't understand why this fog is limited to such a small space. Everything else in the landscape is visible.'

Okura had no explanation either.

'Shall I go alone? I can find my way.'

'Wait a minute. That can wait.' Rhodan rummaged in the bag he had taken away from the 'pacifists' and extracted two landmines. 'I imagine this ought to stir them up.'

They returned to the forest and treaded their way to the back of the hostile platoon. They deposited the mines at their flank and set the time fuses at an interval of 30 seconds. Then they quickly retreated and watched the proceedings from a safe cover.

'One more minute to go,'

Okura nodded.

Then the first mine blew up.

'They jumped up and are running around wildly. They're shouting something to each other . . .'

'That I can hear.'

'And the others?'

'Now most of them have taken cover again.'

'And the others?'

'Three men are running away along the shore toward the west and one seems to have the guts to walk toward the forest.'

'You call that guts? The man must be out of his mind!'

The 30 seconds were up.

The second mine exploded and the confusion among their adversaries was complete. They all expected further detonations from the unknown source. They began a general retreat to the west which turned into a rout with everybody running away in headlong flight. They ran along the shore where they were least impeded.

'The way to the sandbar is free!' Okura shouted excitedly.

'Let's go, my boy!' Rhodan decided.

They took up a new position where the sandbar began.

'Cover our flank to the west,' Rhodan told Okura while he turned on the radio. 'Come back here, John! We've beaten them off. You'll find us on the beach where the sandbar juts out!'

'How in the world did you do that? Do you have artillery with you?'

'I'll explain later. First of all I want to look at you to see if you're still in one piece.'

As John Marshall's figure emerged from the fog, new explosions could be heard in the distance. The sound volume indicated detonations of heavy shells.

'What was that?' Son Okura moaned.

77

'I suppose it's a bombing raid,' Rhodan said softly and dejectedly. 'I've always said that some of these gentlemen on Venus are guilty of gross miscalculations.'

6. ATTACK OF THE TREE-LIZARD

They had escaped the threat of Wallerinski's ambush from the trees. Alas, when Tomisenkov saw the four attacking helicopters he realized that he had jumped from the frying pan into the fire.

The first stick of bombs fell mostly somewhere in the forest. Only the last three of the blasts had hit where Tomisenkov assumed his vanguard to be.

'This is treason! I'll have that scum court-martialed!'

'Take cover!' another voice commanded, daring to interrupt the General. It was Col. Popolzak.

'Disperse in the brush!'

The open path was suddenly swept clean. Only a few pieces of equipment were left behind.

Then came the second pass.

Once more TNT bombs smashed into the jungle, uprooting entire trees and tossing debris of branches and lianas high into the air.

Two minutes later it was all over. At least for the time being.

'They'll be back!' Thora declared, plainly disgusted and brushing the dirt from her clothes.

'What do you know about that?' Tomisenkov thundered.

'Nothing, General. Obviously, it wasn't my army.

Why don't you try to think a little harder. You must have recognized the markings.'

'They were our machines all right, ma'am. I know the model. They're the fastest and biggest. . . .'

'I know! The fastest, the biggest and probably the first ones in the world,' Thora replied cynically.

'Shut up! I'll . . .'

In the excitement they didn't let each other finish their sentences. The General interrupted Thora and Col. Popolzak interrupted the General.

'We've suffered some casualties, sir! What are your orders?'

'Can't you decide that for yourself, Colonel? First pick up the dead and then line up the men. I'll have to talk to all of you.'

Tomisenkov stared after his field-officer. Then he firmly gripped Thora by the hand.

'Come with me!'

She followed him involuntarily to the communication section which for many months had existed in name only. The radio technicians were ragged infantrymen like all the other soldiers.

'Chekovich!' Tomisenkov yelled.

A sergeant appeared from among the various sets.

'Yes, sir!'

'Radio silence is lifted. Get your transmitter ready at once. Connect a microphone for me and recording tape!'

'For a coded message?'

'Damn it! Don't ask questions, Sergeant!'

'Sorry, sir! What wavelength do you require?'

'The official wavelength, man! Or do you think I

80

want to carry on a private conversation? Stay here, ma'am! You're not going to take off into the jungle now.'

Thora had stepped back a little to sit down on a fallen tree trunk. To his surprise she smiled and answered: 'Don't let me disturb you, General! I won't run away.'

Chekovich tested his transmitter, taped a few words and played them back.

'The sender is ready, sir!'

Tomisenkov took the microphone.

'This is Gen. Tomisenkov, Commander of the Airborne Landing Division Venus, speaking! Order to the four helicopters! Land immediately in my zone and report to me! Acknowledge order and state name of officer in charge!'

Quite unexpectedly, the answer came without delay.

'This is Col. Raskujan speaking! I salute you, General! However I must disappoint you if you believe that you can give me orders. On the contrary, I suggest that you surrender. Unconditionally, you understand! Then we'll have time to talk calmly about the details.'

'Have you lost your senses, Colonel? Where in the world have you been all this time? You were supposed to report to me a year ago as the deputy commander of my supply units. It didn't take you 12 Terrestrial months to make the trip from Earth?'

'No, it went a little faster than that,' Raskujan laughed cynically. 'Let me set you straight about our present situation. My reinforcement fleet landed already 11 months ago on Venus. However, there was

81

no division left that rated any support. Take note, General, that I'm the sole commander in charge on Venus.'

'This is insubordination!' Tomisenkov panted into the microphone, hardly able to hold it in his hand in his anger. 'The Space Department has assigned you to me and it is your duty to report to me.'

'Which I'm doing herewith. I hope you'll excuse the little delay.'

Raskujan's voice was dripping with sarcasm, enraging the General all the more.

'I repeat for the last time, Col. Raskujan! Report to me at once! I'm not going to discuss the details over the radio. If you disobey my orders, you'll have to answer to the highest authority!'

'I'm afraid that you misjudge the situation badly,' Raskujan replied, assuming a friendly conversational tone. 'I *am* the highest authority! The past year is now history. You should learn from the past. I, Col. Raskujan, alone hold power on Venus. The whole planet is under my command. And believe me, I've got the means to enforce my orders. Don't confuse your band of pirates with the division you once had, General! I repeat my offer. Tell your unruly soldiers to surrender to me unconditionally. I'm prepared to make normal civilized beings out of them once again. Each one is guaranteed to be treated according to his ability and goodwill. I'm signing off, Mr. Tomisenkov. You know how to reach me.'

The General shouted something about traitors into the microphone. However, it was apparent that the other side had already cut him off.

Then the man whose mind had been sorely tried to the limit, fell silent. He touched his throat.

'You should save your voice,' Thora advised him with her typical lack of feeling. Her smile revealed how much she relished his discomfiture.

'How can a thing like this happen? That wretched Raskujan was once in my company. I know him like my own hand. He used to be a good soldier and there was nothing to indicate that he would lose his mind.'

'Venus does something to everybody. Or do you still consider yourself to be normal?'

'I'm a General and he's a Colonel. Isn't that clear enough?'

'Evidently not on Venus, General. Raskujan has started over here. For your rival, a new planet, a new life. These are the facts.'

'It is also a fact that we wear the same uniform.'

'Maybe he took it off. In any case, his behaviour and the deployment of the helicopters make it clear that you're dealing with a strictly organized military force. His power is undoubtedly superior. I don't have to tell you this. You know better than I that the remnants of your old division are nothing but a bunch of run-down stragglers.'

'Ma'am!' Tomisenkov protested angrily but refrained from continuing when he faced her cold gaze. There was an invisible wall between them through which there could be no contact and short conversations like these did not change their alienation.

Col. Popolzak reported that his troops were ready for the roll call. They had found 38 bodies and collected them nearby.

'We've removed their weapons and their papers and deposited them at headquarters, sir!'

Tomisenkov nodded as though it was the most important consideration that the bookkeeping records be kept straight.

'Fifteen men have been wounded,' Popolzak continued.

Tomisenkov looked at him with irritation as if such a possibility had never occurred to him.

'Isn't Dr. Militch taking care of them?'

'As best he can. You know we've hardly any medicine and bandages left.'

'He'll have to ration them. He's the doctor.'

Popolzak had never seen Tomisenkov's face so thin and haggard as today. And he had never heard his chief speak so indifferently about the casualties. Raskujan's appearance had deeply upset him and had left a terrible mark.

The General inspected his troops. There was no resemblance to a disciplined division. Neither in numerical strength nor in their formation. They had assembled in groups as closely as the matted brush permitted.

Tomisenkov addressed his men, repeating in no uncertain terms what he had already told Raskujan via radio.

'We've suffered losses,' he said at the end of his speech, 'not because the deserter Raskujan is stronger but because he has caught us unawares. He was ordered by the government of the Eastern Bloc to report to me with reinforcements a year ago. We'll subjugate him with all the means at our command and compel him to do his duty. We've been warned and we'll act accordingly under the prevailing circumstances. We're going to reach the ocean in a few more miles. From now on we'll be advancing in the lowlands of the jungle where we can't be seen. The enemy won't be able to detect us until we've reached our goal. The Arkonide prisoner is our assurance that we'll gain access to the Venus fortress. At that time we'll even the score with Raskujan. He can put a hundred helicopters into the air and it's not going to help him. Our power will be so great that he will be annihilated. All battalions are ordered to get ready to depart! The company commanders are to report to Dr. Militch! The transport of all disabled soldiers must be promptly arranged. Thank you!'

*   *   *

The artificial fog had wafted away.

Rhodan, Marshall and Okura retreated a short way back into the forest. The fighters who had fled west were nowhere in sight. There was, however, the danger that they, too, would return to the forest and sneak up from behind. As no more explosions of landmines were heard in their proximity, it might have rekindled their flagging spirits.

But Rhodan didn't subscribe to this opinion.

'The two landmines were child's play compared to what's going on in the jungle there. Those must certainly have been bombs. None of the groups we've met have such ordnance to my knowledge. There can be only one explanation for which I've been prepared long ago.'

'You're thinking of the enemy's support fleet, sir, aren't you?'

'I am, indeed. You know I've always wondered what had become of the armada we surprised and decimated near Venus a year ago. There were 200 ships of which we destroyed only 34. Assuming the greater part of the damaged vessels got smashed up on this planet, just by the odds quite a few of them must have landed intact.'

'And they've been lying in wait for a whole year?' Marshall asked sceptically.

'Why not? If their tactic required it.'

At this moment another wave of detonations rolled over the distant landscape.

'Regular old-fashioned bombs,' Marshall stated. 'Probably from *them*, certainly not from a rescue expedition of the New Power.'

'You might as well put that out of your mind, John. If Bell is unable to come down, no other ship can do it. The barrier of the positronic brain is unassailable. So it's perfectly clear that the people throwing bombs back there must have arrived on Venus before us. And they must have airplanes available.'

The two mutants couldn't refute him.

'Just the same, it sounds incredible.'

'Only because we don't know the whole background,' Perry Rhodan insisted. Then he suddenly became alert. Marshall and Okura also cocked their heads, trying to listen to a faraway sound.

A low, muffled rumbling ran through the air. Not the thunder of bombs and grenades.

'There it is!' Son Okura shouted, suddenly pointing southeast. Rhodan and Marshall, however, could see nothing.

'Helicopters! Gosh, don't you recognize them?'

'Judging from the noise, you're right Son. But they must be flying through those low clouds.'

'Of course. Pardon me, sir, but I forgot for a moment ...'

'Keep an eye on them. I'm interested to know in which direction they're going.'

Rhodan tentatively activated the receiver on his muti-purpose wristband. He moved the frequency selector over the applicable range of shortwaves. The set automatically tuned in when it received a signal.

Rhodan held the wristband to his ear and became a witness to the conversation between Gen. Tomisenkov and Col. Raskujan. Marshall and Okura did the same, since they both carried identical radios.

The short and heated dialogue was very enlightening. Rhodan smiled contentedly but subsequently turned serious.

'I was right. We'll keep tabs on them as long as they oblige us by using the radio. It's typical of the human race that they can't live anywhere in peace! Just a few average people from Earth and already they're cracking each other's heads on Venus, despite the fact we're standing on the threshold of the cosmic world and have to learn to live in it. The discussion seems to be over. Too bad.'

'Shall we keep listening for a while?' Okura suggested.

'By all means! We don't have anything better to do

at the moment. But it's enough if one of us is monitoring them.'

They retreated a little farther into the undergrowth. Marshall and Okura with their better faculties for observation took over watching their rear while Rhodan secured the forward approach to the coast, keeping his radio attuned at the same time.

The helicopters had long since disappeared over the horizon of the ocean. Finally, after more than 90 minutes, they picked up a couple of voices. It was merely the communication between the pilot and the ground station but it was enough to let Rhodan detect the direction. He used the gyro-compass attached to the same wristband and soon announced, 'We've found Raskujan's headquarters!'

His call alerted his two companions.

'Where is it? How far?'

'Just a minute! I'm no magician. I can fix only one of the coordinates with this directional antenna. But at least the direction's been determined.'

Perry took out his notebook and drew a sketch of the northern area, showing the ocean and the 200 mile wide channel, the spot where he was located and the section of the continent on which their goal, the Venus base, was situated. 'Here's where we are. The bombs were falling farther to the south and this is the route by which the helicopters returned.'

He drew a line toward the northeast, which crossed the ocean bay and continued over the land on the opposite shore.

'The second coordinate will have to be estimated,' he went on. 'Since we've several reference points, we should be able to determine the distance fairly accurately. We know the flight time of the helicopters. And their course passed a very critical point, here ...'

He marked the map with a cross and his friends knew at once what he referred to. The cross was pencilled in close proximity to the periphery of the energy screen extending in a radius of 30 miles from the Venus bulwark. It also was close to the place where Rhodan had assaulted Tomisenkov's army 12 months before. There the landscape had been turned for miles into a strip of death where the vegetation was still blighted.

'A huge, devastated break in the forest,' John Marshall said quietly.

'Naturally,' Rhodan nodded, 'the Eldorado everybody is seeking here on Venus is our base. Raskujan wants to get into the fortress the same as we and Tomisenkov. This must be the reason why he didn't pay any attention to the other splinter groups during the last year. He's taken up quarters in the canyon where we burned the ground. It's an ideal landing place for spaceships and only a few miles from the energy screen. I feel that we now have to look after Thora. Thora and I! We're the key figures for entering the fortress. Raskujan must be out to capture Thora.'

'But why would he commit such a rash attack on Tomisenkov?' Okura questioned. 'He needs Thora alive!'

'Of course! He's probably learned from the other splinter groups what the current situation is, either from the settlers or from the pacifist rebels. This bombing raid was only a demonstration with which he wanted to intimidate Tomisenkov. It's so easy to aim from a helicopter that the target can only be missed intentionally. If my guess is right, Raskujan will soon make an attempt to kidnap Thora and we'll have to beat him to it.'

The enemy patrol was neither seen nor heard from anymore. They probably had rejoined their comrades when they were strafed by the bombs.

Rhodan checked his watch. The Venus afternoon was rapidly nearing its end. It was 166:00 o'clock and here in the north the days were shorter than the nights.

'We don't have too much time. Let's get going, men!'

They penetrated deeper into the forest. They knew the direction they had to follow in order to find Tomisenkov and Thora and they advanced at a good clip.

Until the attack of the tree-lizard came.

Rhodan had already admonished his companions to pay special attention to the unpredictable animals at dusk. This was the time of day when almost all life on Venus was awake and on the move. Those who had been roaming all day returned to their caves and nests and the nocturnal animals were getting ready for the prowl.

Marshall had to kill a three-legged proboscis-roach after only 10 minutes. The creature raced toward them with a ghastly croaking and the terrible noise warned them just in time.

'Why does this beast make so much noise when it pounces on its prey?' Marshall asked after he had silently exterminated it with his impulse-beamer. 'It

90

only gives itself away.'

'There are animals who can scare their victims to such a degree that they simply become paralyzed by fright. This is one way of hunting. Otherwise this species would have been extinct long ago.'

Thirty minutes later a worse mishap occurred.

They were marching in single file, Okura first, then Rhodan and Marshall.

The tree-lizard let Okura pass by. For some reason the beast set upon Rhodan.

Its prehensile tail reached down a tree from an unseen height and wrapped itself a few times around his chest. He was barely able to utter a scream. Then the lizard choked him so tightly that he could no longer breathe.

Rhodan instinctively grabbed the short-haired tail with both hands. His gun had already been knocked out of his hands at the first blow. However, his hands were pitifully inadequate tools compared to the strength of the huge tail's lethal grip.

In a second he was swinging at the height of Marshall's head.

The mutant was afraid to shoot although he had instantly pulled up his impulse-beamer. The dwindling light of dusk, made worse by the dense foliage, almost blotted out his view. Rhodan's body in the sling swayed so much that Marshall didn't dare fire. The lizard kept jerking up its victim step by step.

'Okura!' Marshall yelled.

The slender Japanese had already reacted. 'It's all right, John! Put down your gun and leave it to me!'

The frequency seer had no trouble recognizing the

reptile. He could see the threefold loop of the snake-like tail and the lizard's rump hiding 20 yards above in the foliage.

The reptile was known to them from descriptions only. Outwardly it was reported to resemble an alligator and it was classified as a related species. At closer examination the differences became quite apparent.

The prehensile tail was four times as long as the body. It served as useful a purpose as that of some Terrestrial monkeys. Furthermore, the lizard was covered with short smooth hair like a beaver and lived primarily in trees where it even built its nest.

The lizard had simply snatched Rhodan up from the path. He was dangling seven or eight yards above the ground when Okura trained his impulse-beamer on the beast. He raised his sight above the coil smothering the human body where the tail became thicker. Then he pulled the trigger for five seconds, slicing back and forth until the tail end was severed from the rump and dropped to the ground.

Okura and Marshall ran over to Rhodan in order to extricate him without delay. At first they tried to unravel the tail like a shoelace but they soon found out that stronger means were necessary.

They also were reminded, to their regret, that their initial success made them careless. Heedless of everything else they were busy freeing Rhodan from the loops.

'Look out!' Okura suddenly yelled, simultaneously pushing Marshall away.

The raging beast crashed down from the tree. It

landed close to Rhodan and it was impossible to see, despite the proximity, whether he had been hit again.

Now the target loomed so large that Marshall was no longer afraid to shoot. He grabbed his impulse-beamer and fired point-blank. The reptile's body writhed and reared up once more before it finally collapsed.

'It's dead,' Okura declared. Rhodan had been lucky. The body of the colossus came within a few inches of crushing him.

'Sir!' Marshall called, feeling Perry's forehead.

'He's unconscious,' Okura stated. 'Come on, John, help me! We don't have the strength to break the sling. Especially as the tail end is pinned down by the lizard's rump.'

'I can see that. What do you want me to do?'

'We'll have to risk two more thermo-cuts to sever the tail as close to Rhodan as possible. Otherwise we'll never get him loose.'

Marshall nodded mechanically. He felt very uneasy about this task, yet there was no other way. It took all his self-control to set his weapons in close focus.

'Okay!' he finally said. 'I'm ready.'

'Go ahead! Shoot!' Okura demanded without making any effort to do likewise. 'I can see a little better than you down here but my hand isn't steady enough. I don't want to have the boss on my conscience.'

'You don't say! What about me?'

'Don't crack up now, Marshall! You're the one with the cool nerves. If you think I'm a shirker, try me some other time but not today. This isn't the most appropriate occasion.'

'All right, all right,' Marshall said impatiently and took aim.

Both shots were right on target.

'See what I mean,' Okura exclaimed as Marshall wiped the sweat from his brows.

Perry Rhodan was now set free in a matter of seconds. Moaning, he rolled over and remained lying on his back. He was breathing regularly.

'I wonder if he's broken anything in the fall?'

'I don't think so. Falling eight yards on Venus is not as bad as on Earth. Fortunately, the whipping tail end acted like a spring. Only the tight grip ...'

Marshall stopped talking. Perry had opened his eyes and touched his shoulder. His companions understood at once. They pulled down his shirt and saw that his bullet wound had burst open again.

One of the three swore loudly. They were thinking about the drugs they had used up long ago.

'Does it hurt, sir?' Okura asked solicitously. Rhodan managed a wan smile.

'Not too bad, my friends. It's just the old injury ...'

He paused to gnash his teeth for some reason.

'Help me up, please! I want to try my legs.'

His legs were all right but his right arm was numb and feeble. Only his left hand was capable of carrying anything.

'I'm sorry! You won't be able to go on with all our equipment. Besides, it's out of the question that we separate again. It'll take at least five hours to reach Tomisenkov. We'll go back to the coast.'

'And what about Thora?'

'We'll have to wait for them. I know we're going

for broke. Raskujan might get there first.'

'He's sure to have the jump on us, sir, with his helicopters. We don't even know that Tomisenkov will be passing by here with his precious prisoner.'

'I believe he will,' Rhodan claimed. 'They all have only one goal, the Venus fortress. Tomisenkov must come through somewhere in the vicinity. I can't tell whether it'll be a few miles to the east or the west. But we've an unobstructed view along the coast and if we have to wait till it's dark, we'll have even more of an advantage, thanks to Okura.'

They accepted Rhodan's decision and turned back on their way to the coast to await further developments.

When they had come within a few hundred yards of the jungle's edge, they heard engine noises again.

'The helicopters are returning,' Okura called out excitedly. 'If we were only out of this forest!'

'Are you going to stop them?' Rhodan grinned. 'Besides, listen again! I can hear only one.'

'A single helicopter? It must be Raskujan's patrol.'

The noise sank to a lower register and became stronger. The decelerated whirling of the horizontal blades indicated that the vehicle was about to land.

'If this is a transport dropping a hundred men out on the shore, we're lost,' Rhodan commented. Nevertheless, they pressed forward as quickly as possible to get within sight of the open coast.

7 THE CARATA VAMPIRE STRIKES

The battered Space Landing Division of Gen. Tomi-senkov had meanwhile been on the march again for several hours. With his appeal, running the whole gamut from a call to their sworn obedience and loy-alty to the promise of a secure and mighty future, as befitted a good leader Gen. Tomisenkov had succeeded in banding his demoralized troops once more around him.

Since both Col. Popolzak and Thora were thorough-ly convinced that Raskujan was deadly serious with his plans, Tomisenkov had accepted the thought that the deserted Colonel would never report to him. If he had failed to do so in a year, there was no reason to believe that he would do it in the future. Thora could not suppress one of her cynical remarks:

'Well, I do believe that Raskujan will report to you. But he won't ask you to capitulate. Instead, he'll put a gun to your head.'

A little later they met Lt. Tanjew's patrol on its way in retreat from the ocean. Tanjew gave Tomisenkov a detailed report of their experiences. The detonation of the two land mines was interpreted as Raskujan's troops having infiltrated the forest bordering the coast. This circumstance called for a doubling of precau-tions. Also, they started glancing more often at their watches. Pauses for rest became shorter and less frequent.

The motto was 'Forward.' It was imperative that they reach the coast before nightfall.

'Thora, who had recently developed a remarkable liking for proverbs of the human languages, commented later about the impending event that 'you have to pay the piper if you want to dance.'

A great commotion suddenly arose at the vanguard marching about 100 yards ahead. Shots were fired from pistols and machineguns.

'Raskujan!' Tomisenkov groaned – a sign how much he was preoccupied with this problem. However, it was not the Colonel.

It was the hostile planet Venus itself.

Popolzak was at the head of the column with a group of 10 heavily armed soldiers. They all marched in close formation. The first three carried machetes and broke the path. Tenacious and practiced, they kept slashing away at the branches and vines, snapping them with rhythmic movements. And as plants are wont to do, they gave way silently and fatalistically.

Yet one of the plants cried out and fought back. At first glance it was a tree like all the others. Only when it reacted loudly and jumped away did they realize they had come upon a Carata Vampire.

It all happened lightning fast. A Carata Vampire, as a rule, stands motionless for days, camouflaged as a plant. This is the best protection against its natural enemies. In case of attack, however, it reacts with amazing speed. It has a second defence far more perilous than its camouflage; its leaves, resembling fronds

97

of the South American Carata palm, are studded with thousands of poisonous pores on the underside. And it knows how to use them!

As it was crying in pain, almost a dozen of its branches clamped down on the forward group within range of its deadly tentacles. The fearful screaming of the victims mingled with the tortured sound of the 'tree.' The grip around their bodies was as tight as a steel vice. They were hurled aloft and the poison pores searched instinctively for the bare skin. When they found it the fatal process took its course. Sharp barbs prepared the skin by scratching it until blood began to flow. As soon as the tiniest blood vessel of the prey was broken, the venom entered the body unhindered.

Ivan Alicharin was the hindmost of the vanguard. He was a born woodsman long before he went through the tough school on Venus. Instinctively he grasped the man before him by the collar and pulled him back. At the same moment he levelled his carbine with his finger on the trigger.

'Move over, Boris! Move over!'

Alicharin assisted him with a desperate kick. Then he emptied his clip into the treacherous mass of the tree. Soon Boris joined in the shooting and stopped only when the Carata Vampire and its victims were lying still on the ground.

Tomisenkov came rushing forward.

'What the hell are you doing, Alicharin? Give me your gun!'

The soldier obeyed but not without demurring:

'Take good care of it, sir! I'm going to need it.'

'Murderer!' Tomisenkov raged. 'You've killed eight of my best men and Col. Popolzak ...'

'If you think that I wanted to do it, you're mistaken. Don't you understand that we ran into a Carata Vampire?'

The General was startled and took another look.

'He's right!' Boris affirmed. 'We had no other choice, sir. These men were beyond help.'

This was confirmed by Dr. Militch, who conducted a short examination in accordance with Tomisenkov's instructions.

Tomisenkov returned the gun to Alicharin.

'Please forgive me, Ali. We all owe you a debt of thanks. Are you ready to lead the column? I'll give you a few good men for support.'

The march continued. There was no time to bury the dead. They had to reach the coast in four hours.

*　　*　　*

Son Okura pulled his head back.

'You can hit them with a stone,' he whispered. 'It's a small machine. Five men came out.'

'Did anyone remain in it?'

'No, they all left.'

'Good. Let me take a look for myself.'

Rhodan saw that Raskujan's soldiers walked toward the forest. At the same moment he made his plans.

'Come on, Marshall! Okura! We'll give them a well-deserved reception.'

'They don't see us, sir. They're not coming this way.'

'But they'll settle down there. I'm sorry these are our

enemies and we'll have to face them. Besides, we can use the helicopter.'

Now it suddenly dawned on them.

'You want to fly to the fortress in that machine?'

'And why not? If we don't slip up now, we'll have everything on Venus under control in three hours.'

Rhodan cupped his hands around his mouth.

'Stay where you are and throw your weapons away!'

But Raskujan's soldiers responded in the most unreasonable manner. The five men hit the ground and blindly opened fire. Since they couldn't see anybody they were blasting away at random in the general direction of the voice. All their shots went wild.

'You can't talk to them,' Rhodan observed with disappointment. 'We've got to shoot simultaneously, John. Everything must be over in a few seconds. Are you ready?'

'Yes, sir!' Marshall whispered hoarsely.

'Fire!' Rhodan commanded.

They got up and stepped out into the open. Okura followed silently. He knew that the five soldiers were dead. Their blind zeal pitted against Arkonide impulse-weapons could only lead to death.

They ran over to the vehicle and climbed aboard.

'A whirlybird!' Marshall exulted. 'And ready to go I still can't believe it!'

'This stroke of luck was too good to be passed up. Close the hatches, men! Are we ready?'

'Roger, sir! Can you make it with your shoulder?'

'Never mind that now! Watch what's going on outside! We're still far from our goal. Where there's one helicopter, another is probably not far away.'

'You mean . . .'

'Exactly. We won't be able to fly across the bay, since we don't have life jackets. We can't take a chance of getting shot down over the ocean. So we'll have to stick to the coast. It's a detour of a few hundred miles but – safety first.'

Rhodan checked the fuel gauge. He shook his head uncertainly. There might be just enough. Then Okura found a spare tank and their prospects improved substantially.

Rhodan, who was fairly familiar with the model, quickly got the hang of it after he started the machine. Arkonide hypno-training and thorough basic schooling on Terra had served to perfect his spontaneous comprehension.

He lifted the helicopter smoothly off the beach and set his course north-north-west. The surf of the sluggish Venusian ocean foamed below them.

They had travelled little more than five miles when Marshall announced excitedly that he had sighted another helicopter. Okura confirmed this observation, watching through the plastic window on his side.

'It'll be rough if they get suspicious about the course we take. Let's ignore them as long as possible,' Rhodan said hopefully. Turn on the radio! They may want to contact us.'

They didn't have long to wait. After two minutes the other machine challenged them and asked for their call signal. A deep voice declared that he – Rhodan – sounded very peculiar today. He meant of course his comrade who had met his death 15 minutes earlier.

Rhodan made scratching noises on the microphone

with his finger nail and muttered in a disguised and angry voice that his radio was evidently out of order. Then he broke off the connection altogether.

'Let them think what they want. We can't give them the code signal anyway. So we just pretend that our radio is on the blink. All we can do now is keep flying and to wait. We'll have to be prepared for the worst. Keep your eyes open and let me know what their next move will be.'

'I can already tell you that,' Okura said cheerlessly. 'They've changed their course and are heading this way at a lead angle to gain on us.'

'We'll alter our course, too,' Rhodan said with annoyance and pulled the machine portside. The ocean was sliding away under them and soon they were above the primeval forest. This didn't help much since their opponent adjusted his course accordingly.

'Oh, blast, they're cutting us off!'

Perry decided to fly head on toward the hostile machine. Not only to get them into more favourable terrain but it also aroused less suspicion. However, it was plain to see that the men from the New Power had already caused the damage and that it was too late to allay the mistrust. The foe left no doubt about this. He greeted them with a burst of fire as they reached the coast. Rhodan dropped down in an evasive manoeuvre but he took a hit in the cockpit. Nobody was hurt but there was some malfunctioning on the instrument panel.

'The oil pressure gauge!' Marshall called. They noticed that the dial showed no pressure and wondered whether the trouble was in the indicator or in the oil lines.

Before they could investigate it they were compelled to evade another assault.

'Why don't we shoot back?' Marshall asked grimly.

'With what?' Rhodan countered his question irritatedly. 'They've got a cannon mounted in their helicopter – we don't.'

'Why not open the cockpit and use the imp?'

'Okay, try the beamer!'

Marshall fiddled with the lock when their rival swooped obliquely down on them. He threw a bomb which barely missed them. The impact of the bomb on the water detonated it, hurling up a shower of exploding fragments.

Okura yelled. 'Our tail's on fire!'

Rhodan whirled around. Rarely had his friends seen him so furious.

'We're getting out. It's no use. We'll roast alive if the fuel tank blows! Take only your weapons! The water won't hurt the beamers.'

Meanwhile Marshall had opened the plexiglass dome. Rhodan skimmed the water with the helicopter and at the right time ordered: 'Jump!'

Rhodan was the last to leap. It was not high enough to be dangerous but it was hell for his wounded shoulder.

He was engulfed by the water and hit bottom 10 feet below. He pushed himself up. Swimming was a little difficult because of his clothing but it was made easier by the low gravitational pull of 0.85 G.

As Rhodan emerged he saw Marshall swimming

close by. Okura was a little farther out. Their helicopter sputtered low over the surf. It hit the beach and blew up not far from the forest.

The Foe had observed that the three men had abandoned their craft. They renewed their attack with another pass, firmly convinced of the inevitable outcome. Okura's warning shouts were unnecessary. Marshall was treading water and on the alert. At a distance of 100 yards he opened fire. Within seconds the helicopter began to glow red and white. Only a muffled noise accompanied the complete dissolution of its structure. A few pieces of debris were torn loose and fell like flaming torches into the water and fizzled out. Other wreckage was thrown onto the beach where it burned out.

The victors swam toward the land. Okura, who had jumped off farther out, reached Rhodan in a few minutes.

'May I help you, sir? You shouldn't strain your right arm so much.'

'Thank you, Son! I'll be all right. See, we're already touching ground and I can walk.'

'Not I,' panted the Japanese who tried to follow Rhodan.

'You're not quite tall enough,' Rhodan laughed, 'but you'll be walking in no time.'

The little frequency seer soon touched the bottom with his feet. After 10 minutes they stepped on land, where Marshall was already waiting for them. Dripping wet, the three discussed their next move.

'First of all let's dry our clothes or we'll catch cold!'

They stripped and spread out their clothes on the

hot sand. As the mean daily temperature on Venus is 120° F, it took only a few minutes to dry their clothes, even in the late afternoon at this northern latitude.

Marshall used the opportunity to examine Rhodan's wound critically.

'You've been bleeding again, sir.' He tore a strip from his shirt and pulled a little package out of his pocket. He spread its entire contents on the strip of cloth.

'This is the last of the treatments I can give you. And you better not give me any trouble. Son, come and help me!'

Rhodan consented and they donned their clothes again.

'I'll try to call the seals once more at dusk,' Marshall said. 'Until then we should take cover. I've got the feeling that Tomisenkov will soon show up in this neighbourhood.'

'The man ought to come to his senses and join hands with us,' Okura speculated.

'Yes, we could make a deal with him. If he releases Thora, we would help him against Raskujan,' Rhodan declared.

'Why do you want to take his side?' Marshall asked. 'Raskujan would make a better ally. He's got the means to take us to the fortress in a few hours.'

'He may have the means but he hasn't got the will, my boy. No, Raskujan must be eliminated as an ally, even though he possesses superb equipment and commands an army which is in excellent shape. Even after a year on Venus he has ample means but so far he hasn't had to prove himself here. By contrast, Tomisenkov has asserted himself as a master in the wild Venusian jungle. Besides, Raskujan is in the wrong.'

'Do you oppose him on moral grounds, too?' Marshall asked.

'Of course! He's undoubtedly a traitor. His orders were to serve Gen. Tomisenkov. Instead he's playing the supreme commander.'

They continued debating this topic for a while, keeping their wristband radios turned on with the frequency tuners ranging constantly over the entire scale of reception. Their suspicion was soon confirmed. There were many more helicopters aloft than the two that had been destroyed in the last incident. The communication between the pilots was growing steadily.

'It's beginning to look like a major invasion.'

Rhodan nodded.

'That's my opinion too, Son. But we'll keep out of it as long as possible.'

8. JUNGLE WARFARE

'Alarm!' the warning went down the line of Tomi-senkov's marching column. None of the opposing groups on Venus deemed it necessary any longer to maintain their self-imposed radio silence and play a game of mystery. The short and ultra-short radio waves had been alive for several hours. They didn't suffer any restrictions whatsoever in the immediate vicinity of the planet as the energy barrier of the positronic brain prevented only the radio transmission into outer space. Inside the barrier radio communications remained unhampered.

Sgt. Chekovich had been listening dutifully to his portable radio and was thus able to sound the alarm in time.

Tomisenkov followed the alarm with precise instructions, explaining that it would be in everybody's interest to comply strictly. His men sought cover in groups under the dense trees. All the weapons at their disposal were ready. Machineguns were mounted on tripods in position for flak.

Tomisenkov watched Thora with Argus eyes.

'Don't give me any trouble now, ma'am!' he said curtly. 'I won't have time to watch each of your steps. I don't want you to leave my side!'

His stern unrelenting manner seemed to have the desired effect on Thora. She nodded sullenly and preferred not to let Tomisenkov grab her by the hand again and drag her around in the thicket. She followed him voluntarily.

The General went to the radio operator.

'Give me the earphones, Sergeant!'

'Yes, sir!'

Tomisenkov listened to the undulating whistling as Chekovich tuned the wavelength in. Finally he heard the familiar sound of his mother tongue.

'Caesar to Lucullus! Fan out according to plan A! I repeat, drop no bombs until the enemy's position has been clearly recognized. We want to capture Tomisenkov alive and under no circumstances must any harm come to the Arkonide woman. Caesar awaits results of reconnaissance. Over and out!'

'Caesar and Lucullus!' Tomisenkov mocked. 'Just listen to the pompous vocabulary of those deserters! Keep your ear glued to the radio, Sergeant!'

Chekovich nodded.

The first helicopters reached the southern coast as revealed by the uncoded position reports. Soon they began to hear the noise of the engines.

In the machinegun nest close to the radio operator the stocky, broad-shouldered Alicharin was in charge.

'Hello, Ali! Wait for my command. Absolutely no shooting till I give the order!'

'Yes, sir!'

Another voice spoke up in the earphones.

'Lucullus to Caesar! Tomisenkov has left his previous camp. Direction of march is roughly north. Distance from coast between three and six miles. Over.'

'Caesar to Lucullus! Observe terrain with infra-red

searchlight. Concentrate on five mile strip south of southern coast!'

At this moment the first enemy craft raced across Tomisenkov's troops. Nobody fired a shot. The men started to breathe easier as the noise faded away over the jungle. But soon came the next report.

'Lucullus to Caesar! Enemy has been located. Tomisenkov stopped his march and presumably took cover. His position is ...'

'Attention everybody! This is Caesar speaking. Follow Lucullus and fly by sight! Landing Corps Octavian to occupy the coastal plain and fan out toward south! Landing Corps Cicero to jump off according to plan AB! Hold your fire ...'

Tomisenkov furiously jerked the earphones from his head.

'Who was the idiot running around without cover and exposing us? I order him to report to me at once!'

Of course nobody responded.

'Open fire at their next pass!' Tomisenkov commanded. He closed his eyes for a few seconds. Thora realized that he was struggling to regain his composure. This was no time for a commander to go berserk.

Raskujan's forces concentrated more and more on the area the observer Lucullus had pinpointed. Minutes later six helicopters raced in low flight across Tomisenkov's position.

'Fire!' the General shouted into the drone of the rotating blades.

Alicharin understood the command more from his lips than by hearing it. At the same instant the first burst spewed forth from his air-cooled barrel. Seconds later the other machineguns joined in behind him. The furious bursts of fire punctuated the steady din of the attacking aircrafts.

It was obvious that Col. Raskujan had grossly under-estimated the firepower of his adversary, otherwise he would not have ordered this perilous low-flying raid. Marauding stragglers from Wallerinski's group had probably told him distorted stories about the deterio-rated Space Landing Division and neglected to point out that Tomisenkov's forces had not forgotten how to shoot despite their wavering discipline.

The hail of bullets came as a complete surprise for the helicopter pilots, who were still under order to hold their own fire. It was the reverse situation from their prior assault.

'We got one!' Alicharin shouted after the first barrage.

The rotor of the leading machine flew apart. It must have been hit directly in the hub. The helicopter trundled down and crashed into the top of a fern tree at least 200 feet up. The debris trickled to the ground.

As Alicharin sighted a new target, a second hit was registered by another machinegun nest in the vicinity.

'It works like a charm. Keep it up, Ali! Get that big one up there!'

Tomsenkov was deliriously happy with his success. Nevertheless, he remained under cover, expecting fur-ther air strikes any moment.

Soon a single detonation drowned out the roar of the battle. Alicharin had scored his second hit. The fuel tank exploded and the machine was blasted into bits and pieces in midair, causing the defenders to pull in their heads under a shower of glowing and burning fragments.

Huge clouds of smoke and steam wafted over the jungles of Venus.

The General raised his head. 'You all in one piece?'

'No damage done, sir! It's raining Raskujans, gentlemen. There goes number four. I think that scoundrel will paste this in his hat.'

Alicharin was only half right. Raskujan had learned his lesson from the encounter but he was far from giving up his current offensive.

The helicopters in the rear had already turned around when they realized what had happened to their leading crafts. This time the Space Landing Division suffered no losses at all.

'Try to get in touch with Raskujan,' Tomisenkov told the radio operator. 'Give me my earphones and a mike, Sergeant!'

'The Colonel is already on the radio, sir,' Chekovich replied. 'He's calling you personally.'

'All right, let me take it! Hey, Raskujan, you got more than you bargained for! I advise you to follow my instructions. If you report to me within the next two hours I'm willing to let bygones be bygones. You have my word as an officer.'

'Thanks a lot, Tomisenkov! I can't promise you I'll manage to do that in the next two hours but I'll be there sooner or later. You can depend on that. And I recommend that you come without weapons when we meet again. I vouch for your personal safety.'

'Raskujan! Don't you understand that you're ruining yourself? I won't tolerate any visits of the kind you imagine. We've got enough arms and ammunitions to destroy you a hundred times.'

'When I hear the way you talk, Tomisenkov, I feel ashamed that you once were my teacher of strategy. I don't care how many bombs I have to throw at you in my next attack in order to destroy you and your ragtag bunch of men. I can wipe you out in a matter of minutes. You're already surrounded from all sides by my troops in the jungle. You can make up your mind: either you starve to death in the jungle and are smashed in endless skirmishes with my soldiers or you come to your senses and let me accommodate you in decent quarters inside one of my spaceships.'

'Thank you for your offer. Your decadent luxuries don't attract me in the slightest. My men and I have learned to live in the jungle; you armchair heroes are going to break your necks here. Suit yourself, Colonel. I'm going to treat you according to your own behaviour. As officer or criminal. Think it over! That's all I have to say to you!'

Tomisenkov put down the mike and the earphones.

'Keep monitoring them, Chekovich! But don't answer them. Tape it if you hear any interesting information so that I can listen to it later. We're marching on toward the coast.'

*   *   *

It began with a light rain which turned after a few minutes into a raging hurricane. The storm broke up all military actions on both sides. When it cleared up again, dusk had set in. The men swore. It was still three miles to the coast. Each moment was fraught with the danger of running into Raskujan's patrols, that were now even more at an advantage, being equipped with the latest arms and aids in the Terrestrial arsenal.

They continued advancing through the jungle. Alicharin now kept closer to the staff of officers. Lt. Tanjew had taken over the lead since he was already familiar with the territory due to his patrolling activities here.

Two more miles to the coast.

The uniforms were wringing wet and heavy from the rain. The heat of the day was diminishing and the cold night cast its shadow. The men began to shiver. Darkness already prevailed in the impenetrable upper reaches of the foliage.

A shot rang out. Two and three more followed. Then a salvo of machinegun fire ending with the explosions of several grenades.

Renewed rifle fire came from the left, augmented by machineguns, carbines and pistols.

Their echo was smothered in the tops of the gigantic trees. The screeching of fleeing Venusian wildlife mingled in and faded away in the distance. The din of the battle grew steadily. Raskujan's men seemed to be everywhere. There were shots from their right flank as well. The rearguard fought back with grenade throwers, blindly firing into the dark underbrush.

Tomisenkov and his officers huddled together in the grass next to an old gnarled Venusian cedar. The men were utterly helpless in the darkness.

'We're completely surrounded now,' Alicharin declared. 'Our best chance of escape is to remain completely silent. They'll detect us the minute we start shooting . . .'

'You've already been detected anyway,' a voice spoke up from out of the darkness. 'Put up your hands and leave your weapons on the ground! You're being watched by infra-red light. Anyone making a false move will be shot. This goes for you too, ma'am. Please come over here! You must be the woman on whose head our commander had put such a handsome prize.'

*　*　*

Ten heavy transport helicopters stood on the beach as if lined up for inspection.

Perry Rhodan, Marshall and Okura had walked back from their demolished helicopter toward the southeast, where considerable military activity was noticeable. It took barely two hours to cover the six miles. There was nothing at the beach to retard their progress.

The sun had set in the west behind the wall of the primeval forest and the rain had ceased.

Okura was the first to recognize the vehicles.

'Ten helicopters, sir. All heavy company transports, I would guess. There must be room for two 50-ton tanks in them.'

'Then the shooting back there must be the beginning of Raskujan's vaunted invasion. Let's keep our fingers crossed that Thora won't get hurt.'

A little later Rhodan told them to stop. Now he and Marshall too could recognize the outlines of the rotary wing aircrafts.

'They're no doubt heavily guarded ...'

'Chief would you dare try it a second time?'

'Would I dare what?'

'Take one of the choppers to escape again. Seems like a good idea to me. After all they can't shoot us down *every* time. Maybe we'd be lucky this time.'

'Or we could be dumped into the water or come to grief in the forest with a worse end.'

'So you don't want to attempt it?'

'A helicopter makes too much noise, Son. They'd soon notice if one was missing. Anyway they're bound to watch it pretty carefully. I'm sure we wouldn't have a chance to get away with it.'

'Then why did you raise our hopes?'

'Think a minute! What else is a transport helicopter good for?'

'You can fly it or leave it in the hangar. That's the only way it can be used as far as I know.'

'What do you say, Okura?'

The Japanese shrugged his shoulders. 'I'm not smarter than John, sir. An aircraft starts, flies and lands. That's what it's made for.'

Rhodan smiled condescendingly. 'And you call yourselves members of the Secret Mutant Corps and the elite of the New Power! Thank you, gentlemen!'

'Wait a minute, sir! You were talking only about helicopters and our answers were right in that respect. It's a different matter, of course, if you consider parts or equipment. There are cannons, for example, which can be removed, or the radio transmitter. They've got stores of food and ammunition.'

'You're getting a little warmer, Marshall. What does

the pilot of a transport do when he cracks up over the ocean?'

'He drops a life raft with a parachute. Of course, sir, I've got it. We need a life raft!'

'It's about time, John. That's exactly what we must have and we're going to get us one.'

They devised a plan and worked their way closer to the parked aircrafts.

'I see some guards,' Okura finally announced.

'How many are there?'

'Three men standing together. That's all I can detect. I believe they're feeling safe here. They must have heard about our scrap with their comrades but they probably think we're just as dead as their buddies. These men don't seem to be much afraid of Tomisenkov either.'

'We'll keep watching them for a little while,' Rhodan decided.

A little while became an hour. Then they felt certain that there were no other guards around. The action could proceed according to plan.

Rhodan had to promise to remain in the background. One reason was his injured shoulder. Moreover, the three men wanted to avoid killing the guards if possible and nobody was better suited for secret surveillance than the two mutants. Okura could see perfectly in the dark and Marshall was capable of reading unspoken thoughts.

'Come on, Son!'

'Just a minute!' The Japanese wiped his glasses clean and picked up his impulse-beamer. Then they started out.

'I wonder if they use infra-red light for scanning? If they do they could see us from miles away.'

'Yes, they could but they don't bother to use it. You can see that they're smoking cigarettes or keeping their hands in their pockets and talking with each other.'

They approached the first machine within 50 yards and layed down, crawling the rest of the way along the ground. They found cover between the big wheels of the first machine's landing gear.

The three guards were standing under the fourth helicopter.

'Let's start shooting now,' Okura whispered.

Marshall aimed at the tail end of the third vehicle and pulled the trigger. The target lit up instantly and radiated away in pure energy. Screaming wildly, the three soldiers ran away and took cover behind the last helicopter in the row.

'Move closer! Be careful!'

They crawled forward under the helicopters and went down into the grass where they were better protected.

'Stop!' Marshall said softly. 'It's close enough.'

'Hey, you three! Get up and raise your hands!'

Okura pulled in his head since he was answered with a bullet. If the soldier had aimed only toward the sound, he was indeed an excellent shot.

'Keep it up!' Marshall urged.

'If you don't get up in 10 seconds and come forward without your weapons, we'll disintegrate one of your machines. I'm going to count . . .'

The soldiers remained unconvinced and continued their fire. Then the impulse-beamer caught another helicopter. It collapsed and vanished.

'This was the second act. Shall we ring down the final curtain?'

Marshall was lying in the grass with his face down, concentrating. Unfortunately he was compelled to read the thoughts of three men simultaneously, which didn't make it easier. Nevertheless, he recognized a few salient thoughts smacking of capitulation.

'Keep persuading them a little more, Son. They're about to flip.'

'I repeat for the last time. Get up and come out without weapons and with your hands up! Your life will be spared if you follow our orders. If we wanted to kill you we could have done it long ago. Well? Your second transporter will disappear in ten seconds!'

Okura counted loudly.

At 'six' one figure rose up. At 'eight' the two others followed. They stepped forward as directed – without guns and with arms raised.

They were tied up and put separately in three helicopters.

Marshall fired a signal with the impulse-beamer. Short – long – short. It was the sign for Rhodan, who soon showed up.

'It's done, sir! The three are trussed up and put away in the 'copters. Now we can poke through the other machines.'

'Well done, friends!'

As was to be expected, the helicopters were loaded with war equipment for all conceivable eventualities. The life raft they had brought along was well-nigh luxurious. It was a seaworthy plastic boat with room for at least 15 people when inflated. The pressurized air containers were attached and a little two wheel cart for pulling it on land was provided, too.

'Take it out!' Rhodan waved to Marshall who was overjoyed with the discovery.

'I found some medical supplies!' Okura called.

'Take them along!' Rhodan told him.

In a few minutes they had unloaded the boat and its outboard motor, a box of food, several cans of fuel and a medicine chest and stowed it on the cart. They quickly pulled it down to the water's edge.

Marshall went back to erase all tracks. Then he destroyed the helicopters they'd looted in order to prevent the enemy from finding out they'd carried away their boat.

The mile-long trail of the wheels in the sand was soon washed away.

When Rhodan, Marshall and Okura came to a small bay and returned to dry land, they could be reasonably certain that nobody would understand the purpose of their operation.

*   *   *

The twilight hours had faded away into the full darkness of the Venusian night.

Listening to the radio exchanges of the Easterners, the trio from Terra learned that Thora and Tomisenkov had been captured by Raskujan. The congratulations between Raskujan and his officers elicited an amused smile from Rhodan's lips. 'If the men only knew how little I begrudge him his temporary triumph,' Perry said. 'At least now we've the assurance they won't try to kill each other with their bombs for a few days and I'm delighted that the pompous Colonel will meet the imperious Thora head-on. Her arrogance will aggravate him right up the wall!'

Okura expressed surprise. 'I've never seen you gloat like this before.'

'Well, I've something to gloat about. Raskujan's my enemy, which should make my feelings understandable. But regardless of my feelings, Thora's capture gives us a certain tactical advantage. His tempestuous captive could succeed in diverting Raskujan's attention if she creates problems for him. And, knowing Thora, she no doubt will!' He smiled ruefully in remembrance of past performances. 'So far he's been lucky: his sole problem has been how to penetrate the Venus fortress.'

*   *   *

They inflated the boat. It looked very substantial and they were quite pleased with their prize.

Raskujan's invasion army had pulled out a few hours earlier. It had left nothing but ruins. And solitude.

Marshall and Okura changed Rhodan's emergency dressing. With new bandages and drugs from the liberated medicine chest they were able to treat him adequately.

'How do you feel, sir?' Okura asked solicitously.

'Much better, Son. Thanks! With all the comforts at our disposal now, I've no choice but to get well. We'll be back in our base in a few hours. I think the worst's behind us. Let's grab a few winks. In two hours we'll shove off.'

The Peacelord, momentarily at peace, lay on his back and gazed up at the dense deck of clouds. A vagrant Venusian breeze opened a small hole in the cloudbank, permitting a solitary star to peer through. 'Hm,' he mused.

Marshall and Okura followed his gaze spaceward.

'Look,' Marshall said. 'The universe is still there. I'd almost forgotten.'

Rhodan was seeing with an inner eye. 'Always there,' he said. 'Always there ... and waiting.'

BEFORE THE GOLDEN AGE 1

Isaac Asimov

For many s.f. addicts the Golden Age began in 1938 when John Campbell became editor of Astounding Stories. For Isaac Asimov, the formative and most memorable period came in the decade before the Golden Age – the 1930s. It is to the writers of this generation that BEFORE THE GOLDEN AGE is dedicated.

Some – Jack Williamson, Murray Leinster, Stanley Weinbaum and Asimov himself – have remained famous to this day. Others such as Neil Jones, S. P. Meek and Charles Tanner, have been deservedly rescued from oblivion.

BEFORE THE GOLDEN AGE was originally published in the United States in a single mammoth volume of almost 1,200 pages. The British paperback edition will appear in four books, the first of which covers the years 1930 to 1933.

BEFORE THE GOLDEN AGE 3

Isaac Asimov

In this third volume, Isaac Asimov has selected a
feast of rousing tales such as BORN BY THE SUN
by Jack Williamson, with its marvellous vision of the
solar system as a giant incubator; Murray Leinster's
story of parallel time-tracks SIDEWISE IN TIME; and
Raymond Z. Gallin's OLD FAITHFUL which features
one of science fiction's most memorable aliens –
Number 774.

'Sheer nostalgic delight . . . stories by authors
long-forgotten mingle with those by ones who are
well-known, and still writing. A goldmine for
anyone interested in the evolution of s.f.'
Sunday Times

'Contains some of the very best s.f. from the Thirties
. . . emphatically value for money.'
Evening Standard

A MIDSUMMER TEMPEST

Poul Anderson

'The best writing he's done in years ... his language is superb. Worth buying for your permanent collection.'

– *The Alien Critic*

Somewhere, spinning through another universe, is an Earth where a twist of fate, a revolution and a few early inventions have made a world quite unlike our own.

It is a world where Cavaliers and Puritans battle with the aid of observation balloons and steam trains; where Oberon and Titania join forces with King Arthur to resist the Industrial Revolution; and where the future meshes with the past in the shape of Valeria, time traveller from New York.

PROTECTOR

Larry Niven

Phssthpok the Pak had been travelling for most of his 32,000 years – his mission, to save, develop and protect the group of pak breeders sent out into space some 2½ million years before ...

Brennan was a Belter, the product of a fiercely independent, somewhat anarchic society living in, on and around an outer asteroid belt. The Belters were rebels one and all, and Brennan was a Smuggler. The Belt worlds had been tracking the pak ship for days – Brennan figured to meet that ship first ...

He was never seen again – at least not in the form of homo sapiens.

Larry Niven is the author of RINGWORLD which won both the Hugo and Nebula awards for the best s.f. novel of the year.

THE FLIGHT OF THE HORSE

Larry Niven

These are the stories of Svetz the harassed Time Retrieval Expert and of the mind-bending difficulties created when his Department supplies him with inadequate information. ...

Here too are his strange adventures with horses, unicorns, ostriches, rocs and other unlikely fauna, both extinct and as yet unborn ... In THE FLIGHT OF THE HORSE, Larry Niven has written a collection of science fiction stories which combine fantasy and mainstream s.f. with superb story telling.

THE ULTRA SECRET

F. W. Winterbotham

'The greatest British Intelligence coup of the Second World War has never been told till now'
Daily Mail

For thirty-five years the expert team of cryptanalysts who worked at Bletchley Park have kept the secret of how, with the help of a Polish defector, British Intelligence obtained a precise copy of the highly secret and complex German coding machine known as Enigma, and then broke the coding system to intercept all top-grade German military signals. Group-Captain Winterbotham was the man in charge of security and communication of this information. Now he is free to tell the story of that amazing coup and what it uncovered.

'A story as bizarre as anything in spy fiction . . . the book adds a new dimension to the history of World War II'
New York Times

'Military historians, like the general reader, will be astonished by this book . . . Group-Captain Winterbotham cannot be too highly commended'
The Listener

'Superbly told'
Daily Express